"WHAT ARE WE GOING TO DO?" THE GRIPPER ASKED.
I THOUGHT ABOUT THAT FOR A MOMENT. "I THINK WE'RE GOING TO DIE."

Mama Bear was bigger than a small Japanese automobile. Its fur was white with a tinge of yellow. Her eyes were pink and her mouth was purple. She reared up on her hind legs and scratched the sky with her claws.

I closed my eyes and thought about Rachel. I hoped she would find a decent man, raise our child straight and strong, and think about me every now and then with something besides disgust. I opened my eyes for a moment. The cub watched with interest while Mama Bear walked in a circle. The Gripper walked in a circle too. I was in the middle. I closed my eyes again and thought about our child. I wondered if it was a he or a she and choked on the sad fact that I would never know. When I opened my eyes I saw that the Gripper had stopped in his tracks and Mama Bear was looking at me.

A brave person is often a person who doesn't have any other choice. I kept very still and didn't scream as Mama Bear dropped down on all fours and poked her nose at my bad foot. . . .

Books by Sean Hanlon

The Big Dark
The Cold Front
The Frozen Franklin

Published by POCKET BOOKS

THE FROZEN FRANKLIN

SEAN HANLON

POCKET BOOKS

New York London Toronto Sydney Tokyo Singapore

To my sister, Denise Marie

An *Original* Publication of POCKET BOOKS

 POCKET BOOKS, a division of Simon & Schuster Inc.
1230 Avenue of the Americas, New York, NY 10020

ISBN: 0-671-70730-2

First Pocket Books printing December 1990

10 9 8 7 6 5 4 3 2 1

POCKET and colophon are registered trademarks of Simon & Schuster Inc.

Printed in the U.S.A.

AUTHOR'S NOTE

This is a book of fiction supported by fact. We do know that Sir John Franklin and 128 officers and men of the British Royal Navy went looking for the fabled Northwest Passage in 1845. We do know that their ships were trapped in the pack ice north of mainland Canada and that none of the men made it back alive. Dozens of remains and artifacts pointed to a variety of calamities which beset the expedition, including starvation, scurvy, lead poisoning, and cannibalism. The Innuit people who lived nearby told stories of a white man buried in stone and of another who scratched paper with a stick. They befriended this man, whom they called Aglooka. They said Aglooka ate raw meat in the Eskimo fashion and outlived the others by a number of years. The rest is a figment of my imagination.

S.R.H.

CHAPTER 1

It was an especially quick thaw after an especially hard freeze. A thousand glaciers melted all at once, dumping trillions of gallons of water into the Matanuska River. The surging currents washed away big chunks of cheap real estate, including Millie Walker's greenhouse and a lettuce field over by the University of Alaska's Experimental Farm.

I'd been attracted to the valley by the cheap real estate. The market had crashed in a big way, so I figured I could live next to nowhere for next to nothing. I thought I wanted solitude, and would have become a survivalist had I been able to survive. I know little about guns and less about the wilderness, so I took a job in radio. On radio I could be a voice in the middle of the night. No one would ever know my face, and I could do my penance in peace.

Penance is a funny thing. I learned about it in Catholic school back in the good old days, when I could still blame my problems on somebody else. The nuns taught us to chant a penitent prayer:

> Oh my God I am hardly sorry for having offended thee. . . .

"That's 'heartily,' not 'hardly,' " the priest would always say.

I went to Confession on a regular basis until the summer of my thirteenth year. Until then my life was so exemplary that sometimes I had to fabricate sins just so I'd have something to confess. This, of course, was a sin itself and gave me something else to confess the next time around. All that changed in the summer of my thirteenth year, when my capacity for sin began to outstrip my capacity for penance. I just couldn't say enough prayers to wash away the stain of my many iniquities. "Father, forgive me for I have sinned. Since my last Confession I lied to my teacher once, got in a fight with Joey Alberghetti, and had several hundred thousand impure thoughts."

"That sounds like a lot of thinking," Father Brink would say. "Have you been neglecting your studies?" I was pretty sure that Father Brink knew exactly who I was. What if he decided to tell my mom? She'd never let me use the bathroom again.

"I don't know, Father," I would say. "Sometimes I think I'm going to explode. Is it true your balls turn blue if you don't pound your pud? Alvin Kosinski told me that."

"That is not true," Father Brink would say. "Jesus himself was celibate, and so were his Apostles, and I assure you that their balls did not turn blue."

"How do you know, Father? The Bible never talks about stuff like that."

A long silence was followed by a quick clearing of the throat. "I want you to say fifty Our Fathers and fifty Hail Marys and avoid the near occasion of sin. Take cold showers and play a lot of basketball. This too soon shall pass."

But it didn't pass and I couldn't avoid the occasion of sin, near or otherwise. Even St. Cletus Catholic School was full of near occasions of sin, slim Polish girls with blond hair and long legs, chesty Mexican girls with brown skin and beautiful eyes, and Irish lassies with red hair and lots of freckles. What's a poor boy to do? Turn blue or pound his pud. I stopped going to Confession, but I didn't stop confessing my sins.

It's my bad luck that the second of the seven sacraments is the one that really made an impression on me. I think most Catholics, be they lapsed, fallen, or bound for glory, would agree that Confession is almost as unpleasant a sacrament as Extreme Unction, which is what happens to Catholics when they die. And if it's unpleasant for the penitent, it must be hell for the priest. I don't believe in priests anymore, so readers will have to do.

This particular Confession is about a crime that happened many years ago. It's about an Australian thief, a beautiful scientist, and dead men buried in permafrost with poison in their veins.

The radio station I worked at was owned by the Speaker of the Alaska House of Representatives, a man of liberal views who believed in the healing power of technology. The station was completely automated, except for me and the Speaker's wife, who handled the books and dealt with the most important advertisers.

KREL Kountry Radio, 580 on the AM dial, used the services of Kountry Klassics, Inc., a San Antonio company that beamed all the latest country and western hits up to a Westar Telecommunications Satellite and then down to little radio stations with call letters that start with *K*. There are ten thousand radio stations in the country, and every one of them west of the Mississippi has call letters that start with *K*. Kountry Klassics, Inc. makes a lot of money a little at a time.

The Speaker paid them $265 a month for a full schedule of radio programs, including national news bulletins and a Christian preacher on Sundays. The music was played by generic deejays—Gary, Jack, Karen Wilson, and Steady Eddie Miller. They were very smooth and professional and sounded like they were right there in Alaska instead of in San Antonio. After a while people stopped asking me for their autographs.

My job was to keep them on the air by selling ads and tending to the computer. I hosted "Trapline," a late-night, call-in show, and produced several five-minute news reports for broadcast during "drive time," when commuting workers were stuck in their cars and had to listen to something. The news was the easiest part of my job, because when you get right down to it, gathering and writing news is the only thing that I can do with any degree of skill. I went heavy on the traffic reports because cars and radios go together like houses and TVs, because you can't watch TV while driving a car. It started with an early-morning traffic report.

KREL Kountry Radio is located in an old pipeline trailer that the Speaker had dragged up to the top of the Bodenburg Butte, a flat lump of forested hill squeezed between the Chugach Mountains and the Eklunta Mud Flats. In the winter the sun never shines on the butte, because the few hours of light that filter up from the south are swallowed by the shadow of Pioneer Peak. In the summer the sun never stops. It gets a little gray about 2:00 A.M., but not dark enough to sleep, so I'd covered the windows in my bedroom with publicity posters of Karen Wilson and Steady Eddie Miller, two of our fast-talking smoothies from San Antonio.

But the Alaska sun is relentless, and continued to leak through their lighter features, especially Karen's platinum hair and Eddie's gap-toothed smile. The hair and the smile were glowing in the dark when Trooper Kornvalt called me with the news.

"KREL Kountry Radio," I think I said, still groggy from the sleep he'd interrupted. I looked at the clock. It was 4:17 A.M.

"Sorry to bother you, Pres," Trooper Kornvalt said, "but we've got a situation here. We need your help with traffic control."

"What's that?"

"There's some people stuck out on the flats."

"What do you want me to do?"

"I want you to tell motorists to keep driving and stay out of the way. It's a Code Red situation. The tide is coming in."

I taped a report to that effect and programmed the computer to play it while I was gone. I listened to myself on the radio as I drove out to the flats.

CHAPTER 2

The Eklunta Flats were covered with a thick mist that muffled the screams of the terrified men. The sun made the mist glow like Karen Wilson's platinum hair.

"Prester John Riordan!" Trooper Kornvalt said. "I just heard you on the radio. Thanks for the traffic report. But what are you doing here? I mean, how did you get here so fast?"

"You want a quick lesson in the magic of radio?"

"I guess not," Trooper Kornvalt said. "We've got a situation here."

The Eklunta Flats are made of the same kind of fine glacial silt that covers the Bodenburg Butte and everything else in the valley. Just add tidewater and it makes a cold, gray mud that acts like quicksand leavened with glue. An unidentified number of men had walked into the mist and sunk into the mud.

Volunteer firemen had started to gather for a desperate rescue attempt. Ed Hilligus came in his Chevy and Dr. Bud in his National Guard Jeep. Bud said the National Guard helicopter was on its way from the armory in Kenai, where the Guard was playing a war game called Russian Roulette.

"It'll be an hour at least," Bud said, "and that's not nearly fast enough. I just checked my tidebook and it says high tide should be here in fifty-seven minutes. Depending on just where they're stuck, everybody who's shorter than six-foot-two-or-three-inches tall could drown."

"The chief better hurry up with the boats," another volunteer fireman said. I'm not sure who it was. I wasn't looking in his direction.

The chief of the Matanuska Volunteer Fire Department was a man named Daniel Woods who called himself Danger Dan. Danger has a story that I'll have to tell at some point. For reasons that will soon be clear, it might as well be now.

Daniel Woods was married once, and was once the owner of a gravel pit. These two former conditions are closely connected to one another because after ten years and seven children, his wife got a lawyer who filed for divorce on the grounds that all her husband ever did was talk about the gravel business. Judge Gloria Hundstaedler granted the divorce and gave Mrs. Woods the children, the house, the car, the savings, alimony, and child support. After all the lawyers were paid, Dan was left with a gravel truck, his gravel pit, and just enough money to feed himself so he could crush gravel for the rest of his life and keep up with the monthly payments the court had decreed.

That's when he started calling himself Danger Dan, and he hasn't crushed a single rock since. He closed down the gravel pit and devoted himself to a new obsession: the hating of laws, lawyers, law books, law schools, courts of law, and people named Lawson. He cruised the valley in his gravel truck, which he'd covered with hand-painted plywood signs and with illustrations of Judge Gloria Hundstaedler and other local lawyers in compromising situations. The signs were sometimes misspelled, but always to the point:

BEWEAR OF LEGAL BRIEFS
DESTROY THE LEGAL SYSTEM
LAWYERS RUINED MY LIFE
LAWYERS ARE SATAN IN A PIN-STRIPED SOOT
VOTE FOR SPEAKER GERTEVORST BECAUSE HE HATES
LAWYERS TOO
KILL ALL THE LAWYERS

This last phrase was taken from *Henry the Sixth,* a play by William Shakespeare. When John Cade tries to incite the craftsmen to an insurrection against Henry VI, Dick the butcher says, "The first thing we do, let's kill all the lawyers." This battle cry was also the title of a newspaper that Danger and his followers printed every now and then.

Danger's gravel truck became the subject of a celebrated case before the Alaska Supreme Court after a state trooper gave him a ticket for driving an unsafe vehicle. The complaint stated that a particularly obnoxious sign was blocking his rearview mirror. Danger Dan called a press conference and the reporters ate it up. He argued in court, without the benefit of counsel, that freedom was more important than safety. The state argued otherwise. Most Alaskans would rather be free than safe, so Danger Dan won his case. He's been a hero ever since, and now holds meetings of a lawyer-hating club that calls itself the Alaska Free Party. Party members worked hard to get Danger elected fire chief.

The chief of the Matanuska Volunteer Fire Department drove up in his gravel truck and parked it on the shoulder of the road, which as it happens was made of gravel that Dan had crushed before the divorce. Danger's men gathered around while he and Trooper Kornvalt discussed the situation. I took out my tape recorder and pointed the mike at them, gathering sound for the radio report I intended to write.

"We called for the chopper," Trooper Kornvalt said, "but it won't get here for at least an hour."

Dr. Bud pulled out his tidebook and repeated what he'd said before with one major modification: Now there were only thirty-six minutes until high tide.

"Then we better get a move on," Danger Dan said.

He pulled a lever to open the back of his gravel truck in which was packed a tent, several more antilawyer signs, and four Zodiacs, which are pontoonlike motorboats popular with sports fishermen. As they dragged the boats into the tide, several volunteer firemen became mired in the mud and had to be extricated by their mates. Two boats were successfully launched. I rode along in the second one with Ed Hilligus and Dr. Bud.

"I think they must be Canadians," Ed Hilligus said. "I could hear them pretty good a little while back when the wind died down and I thought I heard one of them say 'Hey, hoser! I'm talking to you'. It's funny how those Canadians talk."

"Yea, sure. You betcha," Dr. Bud replied. Bud was from Seattle.

We plunged into the glowing mist that had rolled in with the tide. Dr. Bud was at the wheel. He teased the Zodiac forward with short bursts of power between which we could hear the commotion caused by the stranded men. The mist so muffled their terrified screams that we were on them before we knew it, and almost ran one man over. Ed Hilligus was part right. Three men were stuck in the mud. The shortest one talked like a Canadian. He said, "Hey, you hosers! Get me out of here! The water's up to my neck, eh. Hurry up or I'm going under."

The two other men who were stuck talked in a peculiar dialect I later identified as Australian. One of them said, "Step on it, mates!" The other said, "Take a dekko over here?"

A fourth man looked more like a boy, and didn't say a thing. He was sitting on a big gray rock which protruded from the water about ten yards from where the others were stuck. He had long blond hair and a deep brown tan, like a surfer who had lost his board. He made no effort to help the others. Dr. Bud maneuvered the boat in his direction, which excited a look of alarm on his face.

"Hop in," Dr. Bud said. "We don't have all day."

The young man thought about it for a second and then did as he was told. The Zodiac wobbled when he landed on the deck. He had a pair of snowshoes tucked under his arms.

"Guday, gents," he said in a strangely cheerful tone of voice, considering the seriousness of the occasion.

We turned our attention to the other three men. The incoming tide touched the chin of the short Canadian.

Dr. Bud said to him, "We don't have a lot of time. Five minutes at the most. We'll try and pull you out."

"The hell you will," he replied, without a lot of conviction. His face was pale and his jaw was slack. He was looking at something he couldn't see, maybe memories of a life with legs.

We looped a rope under his arms. By this time Danger Dan had arrived with a second Zodiac full of firemen. They looped another rope under his arms and then waited for further instructions.

"Here's the plan," Danger screamed so everybody could hear. "We go full throttle toward the shore, in the same direction as the tide. That'll give us an extra push." He put on his most serious face and spoke to the Canadian. "You've got to hold your breath for as long as you possibly can. Your head will slip under when we try to pull you out."

The tide rolled in, up past the Canadian's chin. He had to hold his head back to gulp a little air. The tide rolled out and the drivers hit their throttles. The towlines snapped tight, flattening the vertical Canadian into a horizontal position. He may have screamed, but we couldn't hear him. The Zodiacs produced a thick black smoke and a terrible noise, but once they reached the end of their lines they didn't budge an inch.

After forty-five seconds of effort, the drivers cut the engines. The ropes went slack and the Canadian bobbed back to the surface. "I think you broke my legs," he said.

Then the tide splashed into his mouth, and he didn't say any more. A few bubbles floated to the surface to announce that he was dead. The rotary blades of a helicopter chased the mist away.

The volunteer firemen now turned their attention to the next man in danger, a six-foot Aussie with horn-rimmed glasses. The helicopter lowered a rope with a noose. The incoming tide lapped against his chin as Dr. Bud slipped the noose around his body and tightened it under his armpits.

The helicopter's blades chopped at the sky so fiercely that we couldn't even hear him scream, although he screamed long and loud, until he passed out from the pain. The mud and the machine were stronger than his flesh. Just as he was about to go under, the helicopter pilot gave it a little extra gas. His feet remained stuck in the mud's embrace, though his arms were pulled from his sockets, then ripped away from his chest. They dangled from the noose like meat in sleeves while his heart pumped blood into the chilly water.

This left the last man, the tallest and strongest of the three. "Here's the what's what, sport," he said to Dr. Bud. "You're going to yank me out of here." He didn't seem angry or afraid, just certain.

The chopper pilot lowered the rope and he slipped into the noose. As the tide had barely covered his shoulders, he had to be at least six-feet-six or -seven inches tall. Even so he craned his long thin neck and slurped fresh air. He flexed his powerful muscles and pulled as hard as the chopper. He didn't waste any strength screaming, although he must have wanted to howl bitterly when his arms popped out of their sockets. But his flesh didn't rip like the other man's. His muscles were bigger, I suppose—big enough to hold together while the chopper pulled him out of the mud. They lowered him back down to the water, into the arms of Dr. Bud. The limbs bobbed around like pieces of driftwood and were bent in too many places, as if he had an extra pair of elbows at the shoulders. He came to his senses long enough to speak to the blond surfer as we dragged him into the boat.

"You'll pay dear for this, Frankie, you bloody little shit."

CHAPTER 3

A crowd had gathered on the shoulder of the road to watch the rescue attempt. Among them were a few interested commuters, two television cameras, and Stephanie Kirsten, editor and publisher of the *Matanuska News-Nugget*. Kirsten was a formerly attractive woman who bowled like a man and said "fuck" a lot. She talked to Danger Dan for two or three minutes and must have said "fuck" three or four times.

When the editor was finished with Danger Dan she came and said to me, "What's going on, Riordan?"

"Just working on a story, Stephanie. I'd like to chat but I've got to run if I'm going to make the drive-time news. I don't have a week to write my story."

That was my way of rubbing in the fact that the *News-Nugget* was a weekly paper that came out every Thursday. Kirsten loved to compete and hated to lose. Some of her news was bound to be stale, especially a

14

story like this that happened on a Monday. I'd have it first Monday morning, and the Anchorage TV stations would have it that same afternoon. The Anchorage papers would print their versions on Tuesday followed by the Fairbanks papers on Wednesday. Finally, on Thursday, Stephanie Kirsten would have the last word.

"Nobody listens to radio," she said as I walked over to my car.

I raced down the New Glenn Highway and charged up the gravel road that climbed to the top of the Bodenburg Butte. It was 6:35 in the morning when I ran into the studio. That gave me twenty-five minutes to write my story, read it into a tape machine, and mix it with some of the sounds I'd gathered while out in the Zodiac. It was classic radio news, with a few facts, lots of emotion, and crisp natural sound of screaming victims and helicopter blades. I took control of the station from the Kountry Klassics Komputer:

Good morning, Matanuska Valley. This is Prester John Riordan reporting from the top of the Bodenburg Butte. Volunteer firemen staged a dramatic rescue this morning after three men became stuck in the mud out on the Eklunta Flats. Here's a report from the scene. . . .

The Komputer took over after the news. Steady Eddie Miller, the early morning drive-time guy, played a couple of country hits while I made a couple of telephone calls so I'd have some new facts for the eight o'clock report: two men were dead, one man was injured, and the troopers were talking to the young guy who looked like a surfer and talked like an Australian. After I replayed my story from the scene and promised more details tomorrow, I read the rest of the news in the overexcited tone of voice people have come to expect from radio: a plane crash, a new disease, and holy war in the Middle East. ". . . this is Prester John Riordan reporting from the top of the Bodenburg Butte."

CHAPTER 4

The Speaker's wife came over as soon as I finished my eight o'clock report. She did this without fail each and every working day. Her job was to balance the books, organize the tapes, and keep an eye on the Komputer while I went out and sold some ads. She always brought me coffee and something good to eat. This time it was two pieces of German black bread weighed down with too much honey and not enough butter. The food was part of my pay.

"So I guess you had the polio," the Speaker said to me on the day I applied for the job.

Lots of people have lots of questions about the limp in my leg and the brace I wear to keep from falling down. But only one person ever skipped all the questions and told me the answer himself. His name was Wilson Gertevorst, and besides being a radio man, he was Speaker of the Alaska House of Representatives.

"That's right," I said. "Polio. How did you know that?"

He leaned back in his office chair and lifted his feet onto his desk. They shuffled around a bit before settling into a cozy niche between a coffee cup full of pencils and a bronzed microphone. He said, "I know a lot about polio because Franklin Roosevelt had it. FDR is still a hero in this part of the country. That's the first thing you've got to understand if you want to work for me."

I said, "How come he's such a hero?"

I've applied for a lot of jobs. I know it's going well when they do all the talking. The Speaker talked for hours on end in a resonant radio voice.

His family had come to Alaska in 1937, when his native Wisconsin was in the hopeless trough of the Great Depression. The Gertevorsts and other dairy farmers had lost their barns, their houses, and their Holstein cows to the banks, which promptly went out of business, just like everybody else. FDR gave these farmers a free chunk of Alaska, cheap government loans, and a chance to start all over. Some failed a second time, others held on by a thread. The Speaker's family prospered.

"I remember the day FDR died: April 12, 1945. We heard all about it on the shortwave radio they used to keep over at the Palmer Feed Store. Papa called us all together and took us to the top of the Bodenburg Butte. That's where the radio tower is now, but back then it was just a bump of land squeezed up between the mountains and the Eklunta Mud Flats. It was still cold and the ground was still frozen, but Papa made us pray for two whole hours. When we were done praying Papa said, 'The Gertevorsts don't take charity, but that's what we'll be doing if we don't give something back.' He stopped talking for a little while and told us to look at the mountains and the sea. When we were all full up with that he said, 'We can't give anything back to the president because he died yesterday. They say he popped a vessel in his head. But if we can't give anything back to him, we can give it back to somebody else. Knowing what I think I know about him, I think FDR would say that good works stay good forever if everybody passes them on.' Or at least that's what my father said on the day that Roosevelt died. So what do you think of that?"

I told him I thought it was great, so he told me another Roosevelt story about how he ran for president while confined to a wheelchair. "Most people didn't know that he had the polio. That's the magic of radio. All they could hear was his voice. He had a great radio voice, which made up for his having the polio. I don't mean to be unkind, Mr. Riordan, but you don't have a radio voice."

"But I know how to write, and I know how to get at the news. I think I can help you out."

He lifted his heels off his desk and dropped them to the floor with a thud. "Okay. The job's yours. You might not have a radio voice, but you do have a radio face."

"Thanks, I guess," I replied.

"You could make a lot more money working in the city. All I can pay you is free room and board if you live in back of the station plus two hundred bucks a week. It's not a lot of money; just about enough to keep a man in beer and cigarettes."

"I don't smoke anymore."

As he walked to the door he said, "So you're a writer, hey? That's too bad. That's what's wrong with America, or at least that's one of the things. Everybody wants to write and nobody wants to read."

CHAPTER 5

Wilson Gertevorst wasn't just the Speaker of the House and he wasn't just the owner of KREL Kountry Radio, 580 on the AM dial. He was the spiritual godfather of the Matanuska Valley and the actual godfather of dozens of its inhabitants. He was a thundering voice in the Alaska Legislature and a friendly voice to the lonely people who listened to KREL in the middle of the night. Both of his voices were low-key, deep, and always soothing, like a tuba tooting the ancient verities. His primary forum was "Trapline," our late-night call-in show. Sometimes he would be my guest and other times he would be a caller. Most times he would just listen to what other people had to say.

The Speaker was liberal with his opinions, but conservative with his money and always paid me a penny for a nickel's worth of work. My day started at 6:00 A.M., gathering stories for the drive-time news, and didn't stop until midnight, when "Trapline" went off the air. In between I sold ads, answered the phone, and tended to the Komputer. I usually took a nap in the afternoon so I wouldn't collapse on the air.

The two hundred dollars didn't go far, but then neither did I. I laid so low and did so little that I even managed to save about three hundred dollars a month. I opened a bank account and called it my Back-to-Rachel Fund. I soon had enough for a plane ticket to just about anywhere. But where was anywhere?

It wasn't at the top of the Bodenburg Butte. I was pretty certain of that.

The butte was located in the heart of the Matanuska Valley, near the place where FDR planted the Gertevorsts and several hundred other impoverished farmers. Local legend has it that the president had read about the enormous vegetables that were nourished by the rich glacial silt and the constant summer sun. And indeed the valley was home to great mutant carrots and gargantuan cabbages. Even today the biggest news of every year is still made at the Alaska State Fair, where the proud children of the Depression-era colonists display their astounding produce. The Speaker's youngest brother, Andrew Jackson Gertevorst, was known for the size of his zuchini, while Emil Hilligus held the record for the biggest spud, an eight-pounder that was mounted on his wall like a big-game hunter's trophy. The grandchildren of the colonists reproduced at an alarming rate and drove around the valley in big pickup trucks. It was a great place to raise a family, but a hard place to find one. Mine had left me for parts unknown.

The Speaker hired me at the start of the worst winter I've ever endured, which did nothing to improve my sagging spirits. First came the snow, lots and lots of snow piling up flake by flake, until it was as high as the roof of the KREL Kountry trailer in which I lived and worked. Then came the chill—three long weeks of forty-below that made the snow as hard as rock and the ice as sharp as glass.

The rock-hard snow killed thousands of moose. It covered their browse so they couldn't eat, and covered their trails so they couldn't walk. Those that didn't starve to death wandered down into the populated areas, where they were killed by hunters, hit by motorists, or creamed by trains of the Alaska Railroad. Things got so bad that the Speaker proposed an emergency law that directed the state to feed the starving moose with hay. Meanwhile, his more thrifty constituents used chain saws to cut the road kills into pieces small enough to stuff into their freezers.

But hundreds of bloody spots along the road couldn't blemish the pristine beauty of the mountains which surround the valley. Redoubt Volcano did that, by rumbling back to life with a series of eruptions that sent huge clouds of gritty ash into the air above the Kenai Peninsula. The prevailing winds blew the ash clouds north, into the Matanuska Valley. It covered the pure, white snow with a gritty gray powder that damaged the engine of my car and made the air taste like a deep blue funk.

Then the long March nights turned into long April days. Spring melted the snow away, leaving behind a layer of ash and the rotting flesh of the hundreds of moose that hadn't been carved up with chain saws. Eagles and crows feasted on the remains, and flowers grew up between their ribs. The mountain glaciers melted into rivers, and the river poured water on the

Eklunta Flats where it made a sticky mud that killed two men and almost killed a third.

I decided to take my nap in the morning on the day that the volunteer firemen had performed their heroic rescue. Waiting a couple of hours before I went into town would give the troopers time to question the surfer, and the rumors time to circulate. Then all I'd have to do is go over to Peg's Pharmacy and wait for some news to walk through the door.

I woke up about 2:00 P.M., which left me plenty of time to get to Peg's before the last of her chicken-fried steak was gone. Her chicken-fried was the talk of Palmer.

The Speaker's wife had organized things while I was asleep. The advertising tapes were in their proper place and so was the advertising log, a legal pad on a clipboard that listed all the ads and when they were scheduled to play. A brand-new spitguard covered the microphone and a window was opened to let in some air.

"Have some coffee, dear," the Speaker's wife said to me. She was always giving me things to eat and drink and she almost always joined me. Her butt was as wide as that of an old plow horse. She said, "Isn't it a shame about those boys?"

"What boys?" I replied.

She had been talking on the telephone while I was asleep and probably knew more than the troopers at this point. "Why the one's that got stuck, of course. The tall one from Australia is listed in fair condition, but the person I talked to said that he's very rude and isn't talking very much."

"What about the other guy?"

"Now there's a story for you. I talked to Marnie

24

over at the courthouse and she said that he is a very interesting man. Boy, really. He's only nineteen but he already has a criminal record. He stole something back in Australia. He's an Australian too."

"What did he steal?"

"That we don't know."

"What else don't you know, Mrs. Gertevorst?"

I meant it as a joke, but she took it as a serious question, or at least she pretended to. "Well, we don't know much about the other three men. Gert Hilligus says she saw them drinking over at the Matanuska Saloon, but sometimes Gertie imagines things, especially when she's over at the Matanuska. Maybe you should go to town and find out for yourself. I'll keep an eye on the station while you're gone."

The Bodenburg Butte is flat on top, covered with trees, and served by a bumpy gravel road that climbs up its east face. These features and the magnificent view have proved to be a powerful attraction to hikers, campers, and other nuisances. A group of healthy people in Swiss hiking shorts tromped across the KREL Kountry lawn as I lifted my dog, Chena, into the cab of my pickup truck. As we rolled onto the Old Glenn Highway, the black lab stuck her head out of the window so she could smell the butte, or the butt, as it's called by people who don't live there.

Besides being a pile of earth named after Bodenburg, the butte is the name of the semblance of civilization that has grown up on either side of the Old Glenn Highway. The highway was built during the Great Depression, when President Roosevelt had his bright idea of colonizing Alaska with ruined farmers. Because these farmers were from the Midwest, they built themselves a tidy little midwestern town and named it Palmer after the owner of the Palmer Feed Store.

The butte is what collected on either side of the road to Palmer: potato fields, a church, a restaurant, a graveyard, the University of Alaska's Experimental Seed Project, and several junkyards crowded with dismembered cars. In 1970 it suffered the same fate as many roadside communities. The state built the New Glenn Highway, a smoother, faster road to Palmer. Time stood still on the bump where the rivers meet the sea. I like it when time stands still because I'll be forty pretty soon. By the time Mozart was my age, he was dead and had already accomplished many wonderful things.

The slow road to Palmer snakes between the Bodenburg Butte and the foot of Pioneer Peak. Train tracks that once carried coal from Sutton and now carry nothing from nowhere followed us across the Matanuska River to the Palmer Post Office.

Palmer is a German-style farm community because most of the colonists were of German, Dutch, or Swedish extraction, robust Lutherans who suspected me of having secret Catholic tendencies. The houses were small and had high, pitched roofs so the snow would fall off them when it got too heavy. The buildings were packed into tight little grids because the stolid Lutheran colonists couldn't stand to waste good farmland, although the Matanuska Valley had more than they could ever cultivate. The Matanuska Maid water tower was the symbolic center of town and the farmer's cooperative was the center of commerce. The Matanuska Saloon competed with Palmer Lutheran Church for the attention of the devoted.

Chena sniffed Palmer while I sifted through the mail. Bills, checks, press releases, and melancholy messages to the Bush, which I used during my nightly broadcasts of "Trapline." Dave loves Betty. Betty loves Bill. Bill loves Dorine. Dorine loves Dave. These people couldn't get anything right. My all-time favorite "Trapline" message was from Dave to Bill: "I'm going to punch your lights out real quick if you don't leave my Betty alone." Sometimes the rantings and ravings of my special guests and the sorrows of my listeners made me feel a little better. Other times their poignant pleas for love and understanding made me feel a lot more lonely. I waited in vain for a message from Rachel: "We miss you, Pres. Come on home. We forgive you for being such a jerk."

I tossed the mail into the back seat, so Chena could sniff the envelopes. Then we continued our scheduled rounds: picking up ad copy from the Matanuska Valley Federal Credit Union, doing a quick interview for my Friday crop report, stopping by the Matanuska Saloon to see if anybody knew anything.

"All four of them were in here Sunday night," Fred the bartender said. "The young one drank alone and tried to pick up Louise Vandermark. The other three sat at a table and didn't say much. Those Aussies are pretty strange. They got their own name for beer— foaming frosties—and one guy mixed his with tomato juice. The Canadian guy drank a pitcher full of ice-cold Miller just like an American."

Peg's was part of my daily routine. I usually went there in the early afternoon to eat lunch and sip coffee until some news walked through the door. Chena slept in the truck while I ate my chicken-fried steak. Peg was very upset about what had happened out on the flats. She'd been born in Toronto and always watched out for her fellow Canadians. A back room of the pharmacy had been turned into a used-book store. She advertised with a sign that read: PAPERBACKS AND CANADIAN BOOKS. The word *Canadian* was underlined as a statement of her national pride.

I jotted down a note about Canadian patriotism and took a sip of coffee. She brought me a piece of Peg's Perfect Pies.

The topic of conversation shifted as some of Peg's other regular customers started to filter in. It was almost dinnertime and business was lively thanks to Peg's chicken-fried steak, her usual Monday special. Friends exchanged familiar opinions on matters of importance and gossips chatted about other people. I talked about local politics with Barney Allen, who was going to run for the Borough Assembly. Dr. Bud came in with news about a new strain of subarctic carrot and Helen DiMato insisted I do a story about illegal gambling at the Palmer VFW.

She said, "What happened is the old soldiers got ahold of Jim Krupp's slot machines and stuck them in a back room that's open all night. The reason I know is last night my Bill came home with five hundred dollars in quarters, drunk as a skunk, of course. He wouldn't say where the quarters came from, but it's got to be those slot machines unless he went into Anchorage and knocked off the heads of about fifty parking meters."

Peg's customers were talking about everything at once when Danger Dan came in. He sat next to Dr. Bud and talked in his usual shout. "Listen here," Danger said, as if we could do anything but. "The word I heard is that the lawyers from hell're trying to charge that boy with a crime."

"Which boy is that?" Dr. Bud said.

A word about Danger and Dr. Bud: Dr. Bud got the

second-highest number of votes when Danger was elected Volunteer Fire Chief. He was now the only man in the department who wasn't a member of the Alaska Free Party. His mission in life—and Bud was a man of many missions—was to preserve the honor of the volunteer department until another election could be held three years hence. Besides, he was the only person in the valley who could drive the hook and ladder. He grew seed potatoes over at the X-Farm, but I won't get into that right now.

"Which boy is that?" Dr. Bud repeated.

Danger had that faraway look in his eye. If Bud was a man of many missions, Dan was a man consumed by one. "The blond boy with the snowshoes that we found sitting on that rock. His name is Frankie Stubbs and he's been abused by lawyers on two continents. He's a member of the Alaska Free Party now. My brother Jesse just signed him up. They're in the lockup together."

Danger's brother was awaiting trial on a charge of driving without a license. He called himself a Freeholder and refused to post his bail. This gave him three square meals a day and something to complain about.

"We're having a meeting tonight," Danger Dan said. "We're going to publish a paper this week and paint some new signs for my gravel truck."

Peg gave him his chicken-fried steak. Danger couldn't shout with food in his mouth, so the talk shifted a bit. Trooper Kornvalt came in and announced that the other Australians had criminal records too.

"They all served time in a place called the Sydney Institute for the Reformation of Felonious Males. We ran a check through INTERPOL."

"What's that?" Peg said.

"It's like a clearing house for international criminals. Anybody that ever did anything anywhere shows up on the INTERPOL computer. We don't work with them directly. We had to go through the FBI. Could I have the chicken-fried steak?"

"Sure thing," Peg said. "What about the Canadian?"

"He's clean as far as we can tell."

Peg said, "Hurrumph," as if she'd known it all along.

Bud said, "Hey, Pres, speaking of Australians, have I got a story for you."

"What's that?" I replied.

Bud said, "Not now. I'll tell you later. Do you still want me to be on your show tonight?"

CHAPTER 6

I disengaged the Komputer and tilted my radio face toward the microphone. "Good evening to the Matanuska Valley. This is Prester John Riordan with tonight's edition of 'Trapline.' Later on we'll read some messages to people who live in the Bush, but first I'd like to introduce my guest and then we'll go to the telephones."

Bud was a regular guest on "Trapline." He was also a volunteer fireman and a colonel in the Alaska National Guard. He coached Little League and refereed high school basketball games. He'd been elected supervisor of the Greater Matanuska Road Service Board and was a card-carrying member of the Alaska Republican Party. He never missed a game between our local football rivals and attended all meetings of the Palmer Chamber of Commerce. Church every Sunday and "Trapline" every Monday. We usually talked about agriculture.

Bud was involved in so many activities because they

distracted him from the central problem of his profes-
sional life: how to develop the perfect seed potato for
use by farmers in the northern latitudes.

He worked over at the Experimental Farm, a department of the University of Alaska located on Trunk
Road, where it was established by the federal government in 1917. The X-Farm's mission was to be the
scientific cutting edge of agriculture in the subarctic.
Over the years, the scientists there had made great
strides in developing hearty grains, silage, and cows
that remained contented through the harsh Alaskan
winters. One scientist who worked at the farm had
even developed a species of tasty turnip that thrived in
the most adverse conditions while another had managed to improve the quality of milk produced by the
local Holstein cows. But despite his best efforts, the
perfect seed potato had eluded Dr. Bud. Idaho hybrids didn't mature quickly enough for the short
Alaskan summers and Irish hybrids tended to bolt
thanks to the constancy of the summer sun. Other
species had other problems that made them unsuit-
able for conditions in Alaska. The closest Dr. Bud had
gotten was a spud called the Alaska Bake King, but
that wasn't close enough.

This was extremely frustrating to Dr. Bud, who
wrote dozens of learned but otherwise futile papers on
the subject. He believed that the proper application of
genetic theory and crossbreeding techniques would
someday produce the perfect subarctic potato, but
someday hadn't come in twenty-seven years, and
there seemed little chance that it would come tomorrow. This was a source of great embarrassment when
he attended scientific conferences in Canada and
Siberia. Agronomists he hadn't seen in years would
ask him about his potatoes, and he would have to

reply that they still bolted, or didn't mature, or were susceptible to the blight, ring rot, or some other potato malady.

Bud still spent a lot of time in the lab, but the true joy of his life was the Alaska National Guard, which allowed him to take out his aggressions on imaginary invaders from across the Bering Sea. When he wasn't playing war games or fussing with his potatoes, he attended meetings of his many organizations or sat in as my Monday-night guest on "Trapline."

"What I want to know is how come the state is squeezing the poor farmer on the price of milk they pay?" the first caller asked Dr. Bud.

The caller didn't identify himself, but I'm sure it was a member of the Hilligus clan. Dr. Bud answered his question with solemn dignity. He had developed the scholarly manner that people expected of him. Furthermore, he took a long time to say very little, and usually spoke in precisely measured blocks of time—five, ten, or fifteen minutes, depending on the lesson he was giving. He consulted his watch while he spoke and would stop in the middle of a thought to avoid going into overtime.

The peculiarities of Dr. Bud and the dullness of his specialty made him an ideal guest since they tended to discourage our more strident callers. Seed potatoes do not naturally lend themselves to impassioned diatribes. But some people have opinions on just about everything, especially Danger Dan. He called "Trapline" every night, unless there was a meeting of the Alaska Free Party.

"Why is it the farmers are dying on the vine? Because they can't get a fair shake in court since they're surrounded by scum-sucking lawyers from hell. There's one lawyer sitting on the bench and another one prosecuting you. They sit there with the meter running talking about a bunch of lousy laws made by a bunch of lawyers in Juneau. It's like you're in a rat's nest and there's no way out, and the worst lawyer of them all is the one that's sitting at your very own table. He's the one that'll steal your wife and charge you a lot of money for it."

Bud didn't approve of Danger's hate, but he admired the enthusiasm with which he pursued it. Danger always asked the same question, so Bud always gave the same reply. "You're right, Daniel. Keep the faith. Any more callers out there?"

"There's one more thing for all my 'Trapline' followers," Danger Dan said. "There's going to be a party over at the courthouse tomorrow with some real peppy debate. I'll be there with my sign truck and the Freeholders will be passing the latest edition of *Kill All the Lawyers.* The lawyers from hell'll be eating the heart of our good friend Frankie Stubbs. He's the first member of our group that comes from Australia."

"And what time does your 'party' start?" I said to Danger Dan.

"That'll be one-thirty in the afternoon in front of Judge Gloria Hundstaedler or maybe I should call her Goria Cun—"

I cut him off before he could say it, and read a few messages to people in the Bush. Then we took a call from Knik, a small town with three gas stations, a rowdy bar, and too many sled dog teams. He'd heard about what had happened on the flats and wanted to know if it was true. I told him that it was.

"They must have been pretty stupid to go walking on the mud flats when the tide is coming in."

Bud took a few minutes longer than necessary to

explain why glacial mud acts like quicksand leavened
with glue. "It's a horrible way to die, I'm sure," Dr.
Bud told the caller.

The caller and I agreed. "I guess they don't have
glacial silt in Australia," I said, because I couldn't
think of anything else to say and silence is the one
thing that radio can't abide.

We took a commercial break. The computer played
ads for Peg's Pies and Pharmacy and the Matanuska
Valley Federal Credit Union. Dr. Bud took off his
glasses and rubbed his eyes, which is something he
often did when presented with a fact he didn't understand. He put his glasses on again, looked at me and
said, "Are you sure these men are Australian?"

I told him that I wasn't sure of anything, but that it
certainly seemed that they were. I said, "So what's
this story you were going to tell me about? Does it
have to do with these Australians?"

Bud still looked very puzzled. He wanted to pursue
the matter, but the commercial break was over. I said,
"This is the KREL Kountry 'Trapline' and I'm Prester John Riordan. Our guest tonight is Dr. Bud
Carruthers and we'll take some more calls in just a
little bit. But first I'd like to read some more messages
to the folks in the Bush."

Yereth was coming home to Bernie and Uncle
Jeremey had had a heart attack. Gary wanted
Geraldine to return his snow machine and something
strange was going on in Sutton. A person named
Grunelda wanted to make "a cosmic connection"
with the Children of the Cord. Sutton was rumored by
some to be a hotbed of either New Age thinking or
Satanism, depending on your point of view. The
people who lived there used "Trapline" a lot.

After I read Grunelda's message, the Komputer rolled some blurbs about Elmer Hatchet's Feed Store and a sale on sausage dogs at the Mom and Pop's Grocery on Bogard Road. Bud said what he'd wanted to say at the earlier break. "I guess the valley's crawling with Aussies these days. We've got a whole dormitory full of Ph.D.'s over at the X-Farm right now. They're on their way to Canada and they're bringing along a whole crew of people from 'Science Today,' that's a very tony show on public TV. They've got an exciting project up in the Northwest Territories. I'm working on a deal to let them use the Herc."

The Herc was a Hercules C-130 transport plane used to haul freight for the Alaska National Guard. Colonel Bud Carruthers was one of its lead pilots. Bud loved to fly for the National Guard, because the planes were big and powerful. The other soldiers didn't give a damn about seed potatoes and never inquired about their progress.

I said, "Don't take this wrong but I have a hard time thinking about an exciting scientific project. It's like tasty yogurt, a contradiction in terms."

"You're an American classic, Riordan." He slurped some coffee and adjusted his tie. "You'll die in front of the TV set, with an empty brain and clogged arteries."

I wanted to be offended and lash back at Bud in anger, but the commercials were almost over. My friend had time for another quick shot that almost knocked me out. "Well, this one's exciting all right. It has to do with the Northwest Passage, English cannibals, and a boatload of frozen stiffs."

Three . . . two . . . one. I stared at the microphone. I moved my lips but they did not speak. I looked at the clock and imagined that the second hand was picking up speed, as if time gets faster the more it goes by. That's what old people say anyway. I felt like I was getting old fast. Radio people have a word for silence. Two of them, actually. *Dead air.* It means just that.

Dr. Bud coughed. That broke the spell. "I . . . This . . . Ah hem . . . Hello again out to the Matanuska Valley. This is Prester John Riordan and we're back here now with Dr. Bud Carruthers. He works over at the X-Farm growing virus-free seed potatoes. How are your potatoes doing, Doc? Are you looking for a breakthrough anytime soon?"

Bud talked about seed potatoes for a good five minutes, then we took a call from a tax protester in Willow who complained all the way to midnight, when the show ran out of time. As soon as the Komputer was back in control, I turned to Bud and said, "You said 'frozen stiffs.' What kind of stiffs are you talking about?"

He didn't answer right away so I'd be sure to listen. "The dead kind, of course. The Australians are part of a team of archeologists looking for the last remains of the Franklin Expedition, two big boats full of Englishmen that're buried in the ice up north of Canada."

By the look on his face I could tell that I was supposed to know about the Franklin Expedition. By the look on mine Bud could tell that I didn't.

"Sir John Franklin was an English explorer who discovered the Northwest Passage. He and his men all died about a hundred and fifty years ago. So far, they've found about a hundred and fifteen skeletons, but they never found Sir John or Captain Crozier, his second-in-command. They think Captain Crozier might have survived for a while and they say Sir John probably had a heart attack. The rest weren't so lucky, I'm afraid. In the end, some of them were reduced to cannibalism."

Dr. Bud gave me fifteen minutes on Sir John Franklin in his usual unhurried style. He told me about the pack ice, the scurvy, and the futile search for Captain Crozier's cairn. For once my attention didn't wander to other things that were on my mind: Rachel, our baby, the Speaker's latest speech. He weaved a web of facts and speculation that touched a part of my brain that I didn't even know I had.

And like a good teacher, he stopped in the middle of a thought, when his fifteen minutes were up. "But now there's this new technology, and these Aussies want to give it a try."

I said, "No. Don't go. Tell me more. What about Captain Crozier's cairn? Do you think that there is such a thing?"

My guest and friend shook his head. I wasn't sure if this meant "No, there is no such a thing" or "No, I'm not going to tell you anymore."

He said, "I should charge you for my lectures, Riordan. Teachers should never give it away. How else can we pay for our Ivy League degrees? Certainly not with seed potatoes."

He headed for the door, turned back with an afterthought. "You should meet these Australians, Pres. They're a very rambunctious group, not at all like American scientists. As far as I can tell, they're interested in Franklin, polar bears, and sheep genetics, but they don't give a damn about seed potatoes. That's why I like them, I suppose. You should put one on your show if you don't have anything better lined up. I'll try to put you in touch if you promise to do your homework."

I'd been hoping he'd say that. It's hard to find guests for "Trapline." For one thing, I don't have very many listeners. For another, the ones I do have talk a lot more than they listen.

CHAPTER 7

The next day's news was more of the same: turmoil in Russia and skulduggery at Borough Hall. The farmers were expecting a bumper crop but were worried that the markets were soft. I did one story about the Australian scientists and another about the Australian thieves. I resisted the temptation to comment that the valley had become infested with Upstarts from Down Under. The Speaker discouraged that sort of thing.

His wife fed me breakfast and read me the Deadbeat Report, a monthly accounting of advertisers who hadn't paid their bills. The Book Barn and the feed store were at the top of the list, which meant I'd have to pay them a call.

"I'm going over to the court first," I told the Speaker's wife.

She adjusted her apron and sat down at the old card table where I usually took my meals. "That's the hearing for the young Australian boy, the one with the stolen snowshoes."

"The snowshoes were stolen?"

"That's right. Or at least that's what I heard. He took them from the Pay N' Save, along with lots of other stuff, or at least that's what my girlfriend at the Pay N' Save said—a down parka, an insulated tent, fifty pounds of canned food, and four gallons of Blasto. He must think it's winter already. The thing is, I guess it is winter back in Australia. Winter starts in June there. Or at least that's what my friend at the Pay N' Save says."

I said, "What would he need with four cans of Blasto?" Blasto is a heating fuel used by hunters and other adventurers who sleep outside in subzero weather.

The Speaker's wife said she didn't know. "What I can't figure out is how come there's so many Australians running around the valley all of a sudden. There's this thief and then there's the ones that got stuck in the mud. And your friend Bud's got a full house over at the X-Farm, just like you said on the news this morning. Australia sure is a funny place. It's kind of like Canada, only it's warmer and drier and it's got a criminal record. They've got a beautiful national anthem, though. I'd rather listen to 'Waltzing Matilda' than 'Oh Canada' any day. And 'The Star-Spangled Banner'? Well, you can forget about 'The Star-Spangled Banner.'"

I finished my breakfast and headed over to the courthouse. Danger Dan's gravel truck was parked outside. He'd already added several new signs in honor of the newest member of the Alaska Free Party. One of the signs read: WATCH OUT, FRANKIE! THERE'S LAWYERS IN THERE!

Danger was handing out copies of the latest edition of his newsletter to passersby. As always, the type was in big black blocks, all capitalized, and as always, the biggest and blackest blocks were those that made up the title of his publication: *Kill All the Lawyers!*

"Satan has a briefcase! And it's full of gobbledy-gook!" Danger screamed at those who didn't want his paper, which was just about everybody. Since he was screaming on the courthouse steps, most of the people he was screaming at were either lawyers or people who needed lawyers for one reason or another. He used to scream, "Satan has a law degree! And he's fucking you in the ass!" but the Palmer Police arrested him for that. It was another celebrated court case. Danger lost that one.

As I approached, he became less angry and more cheerful. He said, "Abandon all hope, ye who enter here."

"How you doing, Danger? What's going on with you?"

He was full of news, as usual, and some of it may have been true. "The word from the troopers is the boy ran out to the mud flats because he knew exactly what would happen and all about the tides. Supposed-ly they found a tidebook in his pocket and besides, who needs snowshoes when it's June in Alaska? But that's not the funny part."

"What's the funny part?"

Danger wanted to tell me, but he also wanted to make me wait awhile to hear it. He thrust a copy of *Kill All the Lawyers* at a used-up looking man in leather and suede who looked like he might be facing some time in prison. To him he said in a stage whisper, "Your lawyer cut a deal with the judge. He'll change your plea to guilty as soon as he's got all your money. Then he'll steal your woman. That's how lawyers get laid."

The man, who was already gray, turned grayer. I think his knees even wobbled a bit as he walked up the courthouse steps. Danger Dan looked back at me with an angry smile on his face.

"So what's the funny part?" I asked.

His anger softened, but his smile didn't. "The funny part is how can they call it murder if the mud and the tide did it? The truth is they can't call it murder, so they're holding him on a trumped-up charge for the one-thirty call. I might even step into the House of Hell for a chance to be ringside at that. I bet Judge Gloria hits the roof."

Judge Gloria Hundstaedler walked into her courtroom at a fashionably late 1:31 P.M. She was a fashionable woman and quite good-looking, as far as judges go. She had personally supervised the interior decorating of the courthouse, and made sure that it complemented her best colors. The walls of her courtroom were painted emerald green to match her eyes. Her bench was red mahogany, a color which went with her dark red hair. Her black robes reminded me of a nun I'd had in the seventh grade, and despite the fact that she was very beautiful, her manner was no less severe.

She looked right at Danger Dan and banged her gavel very hard, as if smacking his naughty knuckles with it. I suspect she feared that one day Danger Dan would step over the thin line that kept him out of the Alaska Psychiatric Institute, and that on that day he would charge into her courtroom and start blasting away with an Uzi.

The guard led in five guests of the state who were chained together at the wrists. Frankie Stubbs was at one end of the chain, practicing his jailyard sneer. The other Australian, whose name was Donald Montague, was sitting in the gallery, a head taller than the rest of us. He was not a happy man. His arms were tied to his sides with heavy bandages and his face looked like he was still screaming. He sweated profusely and twitched a lot, as if plagued by itches he couldn't scratch.

Prosecutor John Boyd reluctantly addressed the bench in a manner befitting a lawyer who loses most of his cases. Judge Hundstaedler's court was usually hostile to the prosecution. Her appointment had been engineered by the Speaker himself because first, she was Hank Hundstaedler's daughter and second, her opinions were even more liberal than the Speaker's. Wilson Gertevorst liked that. On the bench this meant that she was a staunch advocate of defendant's rights. As such, she was perfectly suited for duty in the Matanuska Valley, which doesn't like laws very much. And Boyd was perfectly suited to her. He was a born loser who'd resigned himself to the inevitable many years before.

Boyd said, "Your honor, there are certain federal statutes at issue here. There is evidence that Mr. Stubbs falsified his visa application and lied about his criminal record so that he could enter the country. For this reason I request that bail be denied the defendant."

The judge took off her glasses and shuffled some papers on her bench. "I should not have to remind you, Mr. Boyd, that this is not a federal court and it is not our job to enforce federal statutes. I don't think we should try to do Uncle Sam's job when we can hardly do our own. Your request that bail be denied is denied. We will proceed with an abundance of caution, Mr. Boyd. I'll not have you trampling on the rights of this or any other defendant."

John Boyd had drifted away from the bench during the judge's lecture. Now he drifted back in her direction. "Your honor, in the matter of the State of Alaska versus Stubbs, the prosecution now requests that bail for Mr. Stubbs be set at two hundred fifty thousand dollars. The present charge is theft in the third degree, but there are other issues here that require the wisdom of the court. Specifically, the defendant has confessed that he led three men onto the Eklunta Mud Flats knowing full well that they could get caught in the mud and drown. The results of that act are too horrible to contemplate. Two men are dead, and a third is with us today in a condition of extreme distress."

He paused a moment so that everyone could look at the man with the body bandage. He attempted a brave smile. The defendant gave him a jailhouse sneer.

"What's your point, Mr. Boyd," Judge Hundstaedler said.

"My point is that Mr. Stubbs engaged in certain willful acts which directly led to death and serious harm to certain individuals—to Donald Montague, Delbert Cowles, and Neil Harrigan. A Coroner's Jury has been convened to review the matter. If the Jury concludes that Cowles and Harrigan were murdered, we will, of course, file homocide charges against Mr. Stubbs. If the Coroner's Jury concludes that these were accidental deaths, we have no case to pursue, except the shoplifting. Finally, your honor, there are other aggravating circumstances. Mr. Stubbs has a criminal record according to the INTERPOL report and because he is a foreign national there is a substantial risk of flight. We recommend that he be held in custody on a charge of theft and that the bail be set at the requested level."

When he was finished with his plea, Prosecutor Boyd closed his eyes and took a deep breath. Danger Dan started mumbling under his breath, at first too softly for me to hear what he was mumbling about. Donald Montague shifted in his seat. He would have toppled over if another man with bad teeth hadn't steadied him. Judge Hundstaedler picked up her gavel in one hand and tapped it against the palm of the other. Frankie Stubbs cleared his throat. The other prisoners looked bored.

"What say you, Mr. Carter?"

Eddie Carter, public defender, was representing Frankie and the five other defendants who were handcuffed together in a row. On cue, he jumped to his feet with enthusiasm, as befits a lawyer who wins most of his cases because Prosecutor Boyd loses most of his. Danger Dan mumbled a little louder so more people could hear what he was saying: "Gory Gloria, Gory Gloria, Gory Gloria . . ."

His mumbles continued to increase in volume until the judge tapped her gavel and glared at him. Then his mumbles got lower and lower until they were little more than labored breaths.

Eddie Carter said, "Your honor, the state is indulging in speculative prosecution. Mr. Stubbs has not been charged with murder. He has been charged with stealing a pair of snowshoes from the Wasilla Pay N' Save. Any bail the court prescribes should be commensurate to the crime with which he is charged."

The judge agreed with Eddie Carter and set bail for Frankie Stubbs at $100 cash-only. The tall man with the dislocated arms was led outside by the other man with bad teeth who kept him from tipping over. Another man with woolly sideburns and a Montreal Canadians T-shirt was waiting for them in a Hertz Rent-A-Car. Danger Dan made sure they all got free copies of *Kill All the Lawyers!*

CHAPTER 8

I thought about Australians with some alarm while driving back to the butte. They seemed to be filling up our most important local institutions: the jail, the court, and the Experimental Farm. I had trouble with the concept of Australian scientists. I've never been to the place, but the TV Australia I saw in my brain didn't have laboratories and rooms full of uninterested students. It was too filled up with ex-cons, naked aborigines, and beer-swilling, dwarf-tossing louts to leave much room for bespectacled seekers of truth. But such creatures did exist. News of one awaited me back at the radio station. The Kountry Klassics Komputer had taken a message while I was in court.

Beeeep. "Pres, this is Dr. Bud. It's about three-thirty in the afternoon and how come you're not at work? I've got an Australian scientist who wants to be a guest on 'Trapline.' Her name is Dr. Beverly Godwin. She's a cultural anthropologist from the University of Sydney with an interesting theory to propose.

She's very smart and knows everything there is to know about Sir John Franklin. She wrote a fine paper on the various stories that the Eskimos tell about the Franklin Expedition. She's a very classy lady, so you'd better do your homework on this one. If you don't I'm giving you an 'F' for the course." *Beeeeeeeeep.*

I cut a few ads, recorded some news, and then turned things over to the Kountry Klassics Komputer while I rushed over to the Speaker's house, which was located on the other side of the Bodenburg Butte. My employer was in his library. He was sifting through a pile of old newspapers for bits of information that would confirm the wisdom of his most dearly held opinions.

"Look at what's happening in Eastern Europe now," the Speaker said to me. "The conservatives are proving that the liberals were right about the Russians all along. Give them a little time and they'll come around. They don't want to die any more than we do. All they want are blue jeans, Coca-Cola, and a warm place to sleep. So what brings you this way?"

Before we got down to business, I paid him two dollars for a bet we'd made. In the winter we bet on football and basketball and in the summer we bet on baseball. He always bet on the Green Bay Packers, the Milwaukee Bucks, and the Milwaukee Brewers because the Gertevorst family hailed from Wisconsin. I'm from Chicago, so I always bet on the Bears, Bulls, and White Sox. The Speaker won most of our bets.

The Sox were my most consistent mistake. They'd won a pennant in 1959, just about the time I became aware that there was such a thing as baseball. My Uncle Eddie was a Cubs enthusiast who announced to the family that I was a fair-weather fan. Eddie was a foul-weather fan. His Cubs haven't won a pennant since high noon of the Second World War, when all of the stars were overseas and a one-armed outfielder played in the American League. The White Sox haven't won a pennant since 1959, but I'm still a fan despite their dismal present and bleak future; which only goes to show that some things are more important than winning a two-dollar bet. Proving my Uncle Eddie wrong continues to be one of those things.

The Speaker folded the bills in half and tucked them into his shirt pocket. "Good job on the show last night, but you still can't have a raise if that's why you're here."

I told him about the Australian scientist who was going to be on "Trapline." He smiled a smile that had to be worth at least three thousand votes. "Well, let me see what I've got. We might have a book or two."

When it came to Alaska and the arctic, the Speaker either knew it or had a book about it. He'd practically invented the study of Alaska history, and still taught a course at the college when the business of the legislature or getting elected to it allowed him to do so.

He walked over to a large bookcase burdened with books of many sizes. Each was kept in a plastic bag to preserve it from dust and excessive humidity. The bottom shelf was anchored with thick volumes on the subject of geography. They were arranged by author in alphabetical order, from Dominik Bruno's *The Ring of Fire, a Survey of Arctic Volcanos* to Benjamin Turrell's *The Great Northern Plate.*

The next shelf was full of political books written by local writers, *The Alaska Reader* by Ernest Gruening and *The Lost Frontier: The Marketing of Alaska* by Peter Gruenstein. Gruening was a teacher who'd been elected to the U.S. Senate and Gruenstein was a lawyer who did not get elected to the U.S. House.

Next came a shelf full of Alaska books written by Outsiders. *Outsiders* is the local term for people who don't live here, as if Alaska were a warm cabin instead of a freezing wilderness. The Outside writers included Jack London, James Michener, and Joe McGuiness. All of them were deluded, in the Speaker's humble opinion.

"Nobody who lives Outside can ever understand the place, and nobody who lives here can write worth a damn. Alaska will always be misunderstood. The shelf up on top is the one you're looking for."

The top shelf even had a title card: HEROES OF THE NORTH. There was a book about Soapy Smith, a notorious Alaskan scoundrel, and several books about Admiral Peary, who maybe did and maybe didn't discover the North Pole in 1909.

The Speaker said, "I don't know about Peary. There's been some questions raised about whether or not he really did what he said he did. But Sir John Franklin, now he's the real thing."

The Speaker's Franklin collection consisted of several skinny titles: *Unsolved Mysteries of the Arctic*, by Vilhjalmur Stefansson and *The Lost Franklin Expedition* by Evander Drake. Two of the books had been written by Sir John Franklin himself: *Narrative of a Journey to the Shores of the Polar Sea* and the sequel, *Narrative of a Second Expedition to the Shores of the Polar Sea*. I picked up *Lady Franklin Visits Sitka*, by Sophia Cracroft, Sir John Franklin's niece.

The Speaker said, "That's one of the first books my family ever had. When we came to Alaska in 1936 we had a box full of books in the back of our pickup truck. Mother bought this one at a secondhand shop because she thought it would put my sisters' minds at ease, knowing that girls had been to Alaska before and they didn't freeze to death. She read it to us on the Alaska Ferry or at least that's what my sisters said. I was only three years then so I don't remember much. All I remember is we slept with the animals to keep from freezing to death. You might have heard a story about that. Some of it is true."

There were lots of stories about Wilson Gertevorst, and some of them were true. He'd walked to school in cardboard shoes and eaten potato pancakes seven days a week. He said, "Sir John died in 1847. He found the Northwest Passage, but his ships got stuck in ice. Some of his men got the scurvy and some died from eating bad meat. The rest either froze or starved to death."

He removed *Lady Franklin Visits Sitka* from its plastic bag and handed it to me. He said, "The picture is the best part. That and the title page."

The Speaker was right again. The picture was a drawing of Lady Jane Franklin, who would have been a great beauty in any age, especially our own. Her hair was short and her bosom full. She had large brown eyes and a round face that maintained a delightful balance of wisdom and youth. The drawing was by Amelie Romilly and was entitled "Lady Franklin Insistent Upon An Effective Search."

I looked at her face for quite some time. The Speaker said, "I think the picture might give more credit to the artist than it does to Lady Franklin. She was seventy-eight by the time she went to Sitka. Sir John had been dead for more than twenty years. They say she never gave up the search."

The Speaker peered over my shoulder as I leafed ahead to the title page. It made dozens of promises in dozens of different styles of type. The biggest and boldest read:

THE FROZEN FRANKLIN

They Brave the Alaskan Wilderness
In Search of the Polar Knight

Smaller type was used to promise smaller thrills:

One Woman's Account of Another's Courage

Or:

Remarkable People and Places Are Described

And, my favorite:

Two Daughters of England Encounter
Half-breed Natives With Russian Blood
and a Certain Degree of Culture

The journal itself seemed deadly dull, full of child-ish drawings of Sitka's buildings and lists of the people who lived there at the time. Most of those listed were American Army officers; the U.S. had just taken title to the place from a Russian czar who was strapped for funds. The few personal notes about Lady Franklin's visit were pretty routine: "Lady Jane stayed in this house and attended that reception at which she danced with a certain handsome American Army officer." Of more interest was a paragraph quoted from the *Alaska Times:*

Among the arrivals on the *Newbern* we are glad to see the name of Lady Jane Franklin. The mission of this illustrious woman to this far distant latitude is one that commends itself to every lover of liberty and freedom. The fate of Sir John Franklin, the worldwide anxiety, everything regarding him is fraught with general interest.

The Speaker said, "Sir John Franklin was a real celebrity, and his wife was too after he died. They sent dozens of ships to try and find him. Lady Jane paid for some of the ships herself. Sir John was very poor, but her father was a prosperous man."

I turned back to the front of the book and looked at her face again. She seemed even younger and wiser than before, and very brave in facing the tragedy of her husband's death. The Speaker took the book from my hands and returned it to the shelf. He examined the other titles.

I said, "Dr. Bud called them English cannibals."

The Speaker thought about this for a moment, then nodded. "Yes, I'm afraid it's true. An American named Hall found a trail of fancy silverware and some human bones in a cooking pot."

I shuddered at the thought. "Personally, I think I'd rather die than eat human flesh."

The Speaker shook his head. "Maybe so. Maybe not. I wouldn't want to be in the position of having to make that choice. People will do extraordinary things in extraordinary circumstances. It's easier to be finicky when you haven't missed a meal in thirty-seven years. How old are you, Pres?"

I told him I was a little older than that. The Speaker seemed pleased with himself. I left his house with an armful of books.

CHAPTER 9

I got back to the station at 7:15, less than four hours before Dr. Beverly Godwin was scheduled to be my guest on "Trapline." I felt like I was cramming for a test. It reminded me of my college days. I wanted to drink beer and watch TV.

I only had time to read one book, so I selected the thinnest of the group, a paperback published by the University of Vancouver in Canada. The cover featured a sketch of a man looking at skeletons in a longboat that was half-buried in ice. The title was in bloodred letters on yellow cardboard: *Some Informed Speculations About the Fate of the Franklin Expedition* by Dr. Jerome Fitzgerald.

The book seemed to be the work of a scholar as edited by the *National Enquirer*. The prose was precise and unadorned, but several of the chapter headings were calculated to arouse the admiration, curiosity, or disgust of the reader:

"A Hero of Trafalgar"
"Michel's Meat Ax"
"A Liberal in Australia"
"The Queen's Cannibals"

I resisted the temptation to skip ahead to the chapter about cannibalism, and read the book from front to back. It was the story of a commoner who became one of the most famous men of the Victorian Age, a period of time which had no shortage of celebrities, as it was the era of Gladstone, Disraeli, and Oscar Wilde. Sir John's story was ultimately a tragic one, as if he'd set out to demonstrate that no amount of courage could overcome the calamities caused by persistent folly.

He made his first Voyage of Discovery at the age of fifteen, in the service of his cousin, Captain Matthew Flinders. They went to Australia and discovered Wreck Reef by getting wrecked on it. He fought with Lord Nelson at the Battle of Trafalgar (a win) and against American President-to-be Andy Jackson at the Battle of New Orleans (a loss).

After the French wars, he started looking for the Northwest Passage, a quest that would earn him entry to the peerage which dubbed him the Polar Knight. At the age of thirty-one Franklin commanded the HMS *Trent* on a bold thrust into the pack ice. His ship was nearly crushed to splinters and his men were attacked by a herd of angry walrus.

At the age of thirty-five, he tried an overland route and discovered the Polar Sea. This is the chapter in Sir John's life that was entitled "Michel's Meat Ax" by the editor of the book. The prose was somewhat more agitated than that of the other chapters, as if Dr.

Fitzgerald were trying to be lurid at the editor's behest.

The "Meat Ax" chapter was about how the explorers almost starved on their way back to civilization. Franklin and his men ate wolf leftovers, their shoes, and some fungus that grew on the north side of rocks. A guide named Michel the Canadian ate some of Franklin's men who had become separated from the rest. He kept their meat frozen in the permafrost and used a wood ax to chop off a hunk whenever he was hungry. Michel was kind enough to share some food with his friends. He made it easier to swallow by telling them it was wolf meat. They ate first, asked questions later, and didn't become horrified until after their bellies were full.

Sir John's comment on this episode was a model of Victorian restraint: "The harsh conditions of the arctic seem to arouse some of the baser instincts in even the bravest of our fighting men."

At the age of thirty-nine, Franklin led another overland expedition that reached as far as Russian America, which is what Alaska was called back then. They again saw the Polar Sea, which was named after Lord Francis Beaufort, an important person in the British Admiralty. They dubbed Franklin the Polar Knight shortly after that.

For some years, Sir John enjoyed the benefits of celebrity. He wrote books about his adventures and toured Europe so that the royal houses of Europe could pay homage to his courage. As reward for his accomplishments, the Admiralty sent him and Lady Jane to Australia, where John served a term as the naval governor of the penal colony of Tasmania.

This last assignment was to result in the great man's complete humiliation. The Australians did not approve of Franklin's liberal tendencies. Members of a group of prison guards known as the Arthur Faction sent agents to London to cast slurs on his manhood. "Sir John," they complained, "is subject to the tyranny of petticoats." This was a particularly vicious slur at a time when a woman was sitting upon the throne. "Petticoat tyranny" was a very serious charge. In Sir John's case, it was a sly reference to the gentle influence of Lady Jane, who was always prodding her husband to do one good deed or another. This was well before it was believed that criminals could be reformed by something other than the whip. Lady Jane was a proponent of prayer and education and a determined opponent of the lash.

The Arthur Faction complained that Sir John likewise had no stomach for flogging, and that the penal colony was becoming too pleasant for its intended purpose, which was to discourage crime. The Polar Knight had no stomach for a fight of this sort, and made no effort to defend himself from these attacks on his manhood. After a while, the smear campaign had its effect and Sir John was summoned back to England in disgrace. At the corpulent age of fifty-nine, he sought to reestablish his reputation by returning to the arctic, the scene of his earlier triumphs. He would lead another expedition in search of the Northwest Passage, and this time they would find it. That would teach them all a lesson about the delightful tyranny of petticoats. Of course, the Royal Navy had long since stopped believing that the Northwest Passage would ever do anybody any good, but Sir John was going to discover it anyway. It was a nineteenth century walk on the moon.

The John Franklin Expedition of Discovery left England on May 7, 1845. The great explorer and 128 men were last seen by a Canadian whaler on July 24, 1845. They became stuck in the pack ice and couldn't get free. They stayed with the ships for nineteen months, drifting south with the ice at a pace of a few thousand yards per year. Sir John was one of the first to die. He was very fat and had a heart attack. Twelve years later, a man named Leopold McClintock, who had been hired by Lady Jane, found a message in a cairn at Victory Point, on the west side of King William Island. The message read as follows:

Her Majesty's Ships *Terror* and *Erebus* were deserted on the 22nd April, five leagues NNW of this . . . been beset since 12th Sept. 1846. The officers and crews consisting of one hundred and five souls under the command of Captain Crozier landed here. Sir John Franklin died on the 11th June 1847, and the total loss by deaths in the expedition has been to this date nine officers and fifteen men.

The one hundred and five souls who made it to Victory Point weren't nearly as lucky as the twenty-five who didn't. A few of the survivors ate bad canned meat and died almost instantly. Other men died of scurvy and other men starved to death. Dr. Fitzgerald tells their story in the chapter entitled "The Queen's Cannibals."

"Good evening, Matanuska Valley and all you lonelies in the Bush. This is Prester John Riordan with the KREL Kountry Radio 'Trapline.' Later on we'll have some messages to those folks who don't have any phones, but first I'd like to introduce a very special guest from the Land Down Under. Dr. Beverly

Godwin teaches cultural anthropology at the University of Sydney in Australia, which is about as far south as we are north. The good Dr. Godwin is a member of a distinguished scientific expedition that's on its way to the Canadian Arctic. They are looking for some—fee-fie-fo-fum—bones of some famous Englishmen. We'll go to the phones in just a minute, but first I'd like to ask Dr. Godwin a question of my own. Is it true that Sir John Franklin's men resorted to cannibalism?"

The anthropologist had long legs and big shoulders, but there was no mistaking her for a man. She had the cool, confident manner of a woman who is used to getting her way, especially where men are concerned. She nodded at the microphone and said, "Cannibalism is a part of the story that seems to be very much overrated by you Yanks. Yes, it's true that some men resorted to eating human flesh, but maybe you would too if you hadn't eaten in a few months. Cannibalism is nothing new, Mr. Riordan. The Aztec Indians did it and so did homo erectus, a prehistoric cousin of man. Cannibalism on the Franklin Expedition is mostly of interest to you journalists. For some reason people like to read about it while waiting in line at the grocery store. But we're not interested in making disgusting headlines for your tabloid American newspapers. This is an expedition of scientific discovery. I'd much rather talk about science."

"Okay. Let's talk about science. What are you trying to learn?"

Dr. Godwin nodded at the microphone, as if she were talking to it and not me. "I've been studying the Eskimo legends about the Franklin Expedition. They talk about a white man they called Aglooka who ate raw meat and scribbled things down in a little book.

We believe Aglooka was Captain Crozier and that he learned how to live like an Eskimo. All of the previous digs have looked to the south, in the direction of mainland Canada. But the legends say he was walking to the north, hoping to make contact with a Scottish whaling boat. That's where we're going to look, starting with the coast of King William Island. We've got some new technology that will help us retrace his steps. We hope to find any papers that Captain Crozier left behind. They should tell us a lot about what went wrong with the Franklin Expedition."

I wanted to say, "Cannibalism. That's what went wrong." But the telephone rang before I could. It was Danger Dan.

"Did this John Franklin guy have a lawyer?" he asked.

Dr. Godwin gave me a funny look as she replied, "I really don't know. Why do you ask?"

Danger had promised me he'd be brief, but he didn't promise to shorten his speech. Instead, he gave her the same old lecture, but recited it with the rapid-fire delivery of an auctioneer.

"Because while this Sir John Franklin was freezing his butt off and discovering things, his lawyer was probably back home in England trying to talk Lady Jane into getting a divorce so they could steal his money and his children and leave him with nothing but a gravel pit and a shovel so he could pay off all the child support."

Dr. Godwin made the mistake of saying, "Gravel pit?"

Danger took another deep breath and gave her another earful. "That's right, a gravel pit. Where you make a hard life by crushing stones just like it says in the Bible. She got my kids, the lawyers got my money, and I got the gravel pit. And the Lord said to Israel, 'You have broken my Covenant so I will send a plague of lawyers to infest the Earth, and they will drink of your blood before the bar.'"

I hung up the phone and said, "On that note we'll take a commercial break and then we'll be right back with some messages to the Bush."

I read a few "Trapline" messages and sold a few local products before asking a question that Dr. Godwin told me I should ask. "What's this new technology that you mentioned before in your opening remarks?"

"I'm glad you asked me that, Mr. Riordan. It gives me the opportunity to thank Petco, one of your Yank oil companies. They're going to let us use their Vibroseise Device to help us find out what went wrong with the Franklin Expedition."

"And just what is a Vibroseise Device?"

Dr. Godwin explained that it was a huge pile driver wired for sound. It pounded the ground with a reinforced steel battering ram and then listened to the turbulence this caused thousands of feet below the surface. It helped Petco and other companies determine whether or not there might be oil down below. "It will help us locate certain subsurface artifacts that may have been used by the Franklin Expedition—books, tools, and kitchen utensils, things of that sort. 'Science Today' is making a film for Yank TV."

A man called from Willow to complain about the Vibroseise Device. "I heard it's run by a bunch of Mexicans. It's not right to hire Mexicans when there's Alaskans who don't have jobs."

Things quieted down after this call, so I asked the question I couldn't ask before. "You said before that something went wrong with the Franklin Expedition. What went wrong? Cannibalism?"

There was dead air while she thought about it for a while. "Not at all, Mr. Riordan. The cannibalism was just a part of a general lunacy that seemed to possess the Franklin Expedition. They made a number of serious mistakes that we simply can't explain. First they got stuck in the pack ice. Franklin should have known better. It had happened to him before. After that they stayed with the ships for nineteen whole months, floating along with the pack ice. That was another serious mistake. They could have walked out if they'd started right away. Finally, when they did leave the ships, they dragged along hundreds of pounds of unnecessary baggage—a writing table and heavy silverware, as if they were moving to a new home instead of running for their lives . . ."

She kept talking, but I didn't hear her. My thoughts were occupied with the absurd image of 105 Englishmen eating one another with fine utensils. "Excuse me, sir, but would you pass me the Lieutenant Irving. His thigh is simply superb."

". . . have several theories as to what went wrong. Some of my colleagues at the University of Vancouver think the men may have gotten lead poisoning from eating canned meat. Lead poisoning can make you crazy, so maybe that's what happened. But Dr. Vilhjalmur Stefansson thinks the men all got scurvy because they cooked their meat instead of eating it raw. Scurvy can make you crazy too. Other scientists have other theories, but we won't know for sure until we find some concrete evidence, like that little book that Captain Crozier was scribbling in. The Eskimo legends talk about a white man named Aglooka, and how he scribbled things down in a little black book.

That's what we hope to find with this new technology."

Then she added, as an afterthought, "Of course, you've got to be careful when you're dealing with Eskimo stories. They are a courteous people and they tell you what they think you want to hear. The stories they tell about Captain Crozier might just be stories and nothing more."

She wanted to say more and I wanted to hear more, but the phone rang and a caller came on the line. He had an Australian accent and said his name was Frankie Stubbs. It was the deadly thief with the snowshoes. I'd always suspected that many of my callers were inmates of the Palmer Correctional Center. I'd gone there once with the Speaker and noticed that the place had several radios, one telephone, and plenty of nothing to do.

Frankie Stubbs said, "I'm the one that got arrested for taking a little walk in the mud. You Yanks got too many laws, and too many lawyers, I would guess. What I want to know is where does Dr. Godwin get the right to go digging up a dead man's bones? I seen what happened the last time they found one of Sir Johns blokes. They dug him up and chopped off a piece and sent it to Vancouver for tests. That's not right. A man should be allowed to rest in peace, especially when he's been dead for more than a hundred years."

Dr. Godwin seemed to be suffering from an agonizing combination of anger and embarrassment. "That's your opinion, Mr. Stubbs. And your opinion happens to be wrong. We are on a mission of discovery, just like Sir John in 1847. If we find any remains they will be accorded all due respect, examined for data and then put back into the permafrost. The tiniest of tissue samples will tell us all we need to know about lead poisoning or anything else on the Franklin Expedition. If we find any sign of Captain Crozier, we're going to learn a lot."

"You won't learn nothing. You ain't got the juice."

"I do so have the juice. I've written many scholarly papers on the subject."

"No, you don't."

"Yes, I do."

"No, you . . ."

I switched off the telephone uplink and turned to my guest. She tried to smile but couldn't. It was ten minutes to midnight, and the dead air hung heavy over KREL Kountry Radio. Dead air is exactly that, radio that has been killed by human error or technical difficulties. Dr. Godwin seemed to be on the verge of some very unscholarly tears. I didn't know what to say, so I signed off "Trapline" and turned over control of the studio to the Kountry Klassics Komputer. It was a shaky break because the satellite beam from Houston was in the middle of some cowboy blues by k. d. lang, a country girl from Canada who looks like a city boy.

CHAPTER 10

Thursday, the next day, was a good day for Stephanie Kirsten, a great day for Frankie Stubbs, and a lousy day for me.

It started out like most days. I woke up at 5:30 and broadcast the drive-time news. I led with a story about Frankie's day in court and filled up the rest of the time with rewrites from the Associated Press. There was bad news in Africa and good news in Eastern Europe. Most stock analysts believed the Dow Jones Industrial Average would do something or other.

The Speaker's wife fed me coffee and sausage with too much grease and more of that German black bread while I read this week's edition of the *Matanuska News-Nugget*. Thursday is news day for Stephanie Kirsten and the other thirtysomething women who put out the valley's only newspaper.

Every newspaper should have a motto. Some are more forthright than others. I once worked at a paper in Chicago that displayed its founder's credo in italic type in a box on the editorial page: *Our mission: To serve God, tell the truth, and make money.* I always thought it should have an asterisk with the footnote: "Although not necessarily in that order." The *News-Nugget* called itself Alaska's Biggest Small-Town Paper.

This week's edition certainly qualified. Stephanie and her troop were all over the mud flats story: pictures of the rescue, pictures of Frankie in court, experts explaining why the mud is dangerous, and Chief Danger Dan Woods of the Matanuska Volunteer Fire Department warning the children to stay away. There was a long story recounting the events I've described thus far and a shorter story that reported things I didn't know. Stephanie wrote this one herself and announced it in big black type across the top of page one:

MUD FLATS CLAIM LIFE OF AUSTRALIAN MOBSTER

By Stephanie Kirsten
News-Nugget Staff

Their names weren't mud, but their killer was. The Eklunta Flats claimed other victims Monday morning. Neil Harrigan and Delbert Cowles were the fourth and fifth persons in the last ten years to die after getting stuck in the mud.

But this case is quite different from the other ones. The other victims were young children playing a dangerous game. Cowles was a thirty-one-year-old Australian with a long criminal record. He is believed to be a member of the Ned Kelly Gang, an organization of Australian criminals.

"We believe that Mr. Cowles was, in effect, the

victim of a mob hit," said a knowledgeable source in the district attorney's office. "We believe that Mr. Stubbs led him and others onto the flats knowing full well that the tide was coming in and that wet mud presents a significant hazard to pedestrians."

Mr. Stubbs is Frankie Stubbs, who was arrested on charges of theft but may face more serious charges once the Coroner's Jury issues an opinion on the cause of Cowles's death. (See related story elsewhere on this page.)

Stubbs could not be reached for comment. Edward Carter, the public defender representing him, said the state is harassing his client. "There will be no charge of murder because Delbert Cowles and Neil Harrigan weren't murdered. They were the victims of an unfortunate accident. It's not my client's fault."

Harrigan is a Canadian who works as a charter pilot. Harrigan doesn't have a criminal record.

A third victim, identified as Donald Montague, is also a member of the Ned Kelly Gang, according to official sources. He's been convicted in Australia of manslaughter and theft. He was treated and released from Valley Hospital for injuries suffered during his rescue from the mud. Hospital officials said he'd been treated for a number of torn muscles, two dislocated arms, and multiple fractures.

The Coroner's Jury was scheduled to meet Thursday afternoon to determine an official cause of death. A complete report on their ruling will be featured in next week's edition of the *Matanuska News-Nugget*.

Everybody at Peg's Pies and Pharmacy knew that Stephanie's "knowledgeable source in the district attorney's office" was none other than Prosecutor

Boyd. Seven years before the bench of Judge Gloria Hundstaedler had taught him to try his cases in the media instead of in the courts, since in the courts he almost always lost.

The case of Frankie Stubbs was no exception to this rule. That afternoon, to no one's surprise, the Coroner's Jury ruled that the two deaths were the result of an accident of mud and tide. They made no mention of Frankie Stubbs, but did comment favorably on the efforts of the Matanuska Volunteer Fire Department to rescue the doomed visitors. Despite his unattributed comments in this week's edition of the *News-Nugget,* the prosecutor was no doubt secretly relieved by the decision of the Coroner's Jury. Otherwise he would have spent the better part of a year researching and rehearsing a case he would surely lose anyway.

Still, no one at Peg's Pies and Pharmacy doubted that it was murder. The people of Palmer had never had a perfect crime before, and they weren't about to drop the case without some more discussion of the matter.

"That's one smart kid," Peg said. "Who would have ever thought you could walk on mud using snowshoes? Same principle applies as on snow, I guess."

Speculation turned to possible motives. Trooper Kornvalt said they must have been fighting over drugs or loot. Ed Hilligus wasn't so sure. "It seems to me that this is a pretty unlikely place for Aussies to be carrying on. Why would they bring their monkey business here?"

Dr. Bud was being very quiet. He had a puzzled look on his face. I said, "I think Bud knows something. How about it, Bud? You've got Australian friends. Are the scientists as crazy as the crooks?"

I think he was going to answer in the affirmative, but he never got the chance. While he was thinking it over, Danger Dan stormed in the place, ordered the sausage and sauerkraut, and got directly down to business. "Did you see the new sign on my gravel truck?" he said to me.

We were all obliged to stand up and look out the window. The new sign featured green letters on a glossy pink background:

FRANKIE STUBBS TOLD THE TRUTH ON KREL
RADIO SO THE LAW-SCIENCE-NEWS WHORES
OF AMERICA DISCONNECTED HIS TELEPHONE

It was all very friendly. Danger bought me a piece of one of Peg's Perfect Pies. As I ate it he said: "I understand that you're just a cog in the great Hell on Wheels that the news machine has become. You heard what Frankie said on your show last night, about laws and lawyers in America, that we got too many of either. That's what I've been trying to say. You understand my point. I'm pretty sure that the news whores of America pulled the plug on Frankie just when he was getting to the truth. It was funny how he went off the air right in the middle of a sentence, and, then we're hearing a cowboy song by k. d. lang. She's a Canadian singer that sounds like a girl and looks like a boy. I wonder if she's got a secret law degree?"

Danger said he was painting another sign to go with the one he'd painted this morning. He said the new sign would read:

THE LAW-SCIENCE-NEWS WHORES OF AMERICA
DEFILE THE LAST REMAINS OF DEAD HEROES
JUST SO THEY CAN FEED OFF THEIR FROZEN FLESH

Or words to that effect. Danger wasn't sure if *the last remains* were the best words he could find. "Maybe I'll say 'The lead-poisoned body' instead. I'll have to think about that."

Danger Dan and the Alaska Free Party are a force to be reckoned with in the Matanuska Valley. The Speaker, of course, has been reckoning with forces all of his adult life. He knows when to push, when to pull, and when to step aside. He called me at the station. "I'm over here in my office with my good friend Danger Dan Woods and a gentleman by the name of Frankie Stubbs who is visiting us from Australia. They want some equal time to respond to something that was said on your show last night. Just what was said anyway?"

I gave the Speaker the highlights of the Dr. Godwin broadcast. He knew all about the scientific expedition and was curious about Frankie's complaints. "Can you think of any reason that he shouldn't be on the show? You know my thinking about "Trapline.'"

When the Speaker hired me, he described "Trapline" as "A Bazaar of the Bizarre"—a marketplace of strange ideas. "Good ideas start out on the fringe," he said, "and they work their way into the middle."

"What about the bad ideas?" I said.

"The bad ones are best discussed in public, so everybody can see just how bad they are."

The Speaker also wanted "Trapline" to be a place for crazy people to blow off a little steam. He was convinced that it not only made for interesting radio, but also promoted the public safety by providing a harmless outlet for their hostility. It was therapy for crazy people who couldn't afford psychiatrists.

"Danger Dan isn't going to blow up the courthouse as long as he's calling in to 'Trapline.' It's when he stops calling in that the lawyers ought to worry about," the Speaker said one time.

Among my more eccentric guests were Eloise Kruger, a sun worshipper, and Leroy Wallace, who believed that most of the world's problems could be solved by a combination of strong drugs and prayer. Then there was Alvin Gutenberg, an inventor of many things, none of which seemed to work. These people probably would have been good for ratings, if KREL Kountry Radio had been big enough to have any ratings.

My employer was particularly fond of guests whose political views were in conflict with his own. These include right-wingers, antifluoridation activists, particle beam enthusiasts, proponents of Alaska's secession from the Union, and conspiracy theorists of every shade and stripe, Danger Dan included. He liked the conspiracy theorists so much that he would often call up the show himself to set them straight about something or other. It gave him the chance to use one of his favorite lines: "The problem with you conspiracy people is that you have an insufficient appreciation of the role of chaos in human affairs. Manipulating global politics is like juggling sticks of dynamite. It's as much a matter of luck as skill."

Peculiar guests invited peculiar callers. The president of the Child Support Defense Foundation called about once a week, any time my guest had anything to do with divorce, children, or women. Emil Noovik called whenever my guest talked about fish, politics, or Alaska Natives because Emil was a politically connected Alaska Native who'd sued the state over fishing rights twenty years before. Familiar people with familiar complaints. Now comes the Australian criminal.

"Meet us over at my place," the Speaker said to me. "Emily'll make us some coffee and then you, me, and Mr. Stubbs can have a sit-down meeting to talk things over. I'm looking for you to put him on tonight's show unless you have some objection that makes any sense."

The Speaker lived in proletarian splendor. His house was simple but sturdy and decoration was kept to a minimum. He chopped his own firewood to keep the place warm and hunted moose and caribou so his family would have plenty of fresh meat for the cost of a hunting license. These and other economies allowed him to spend nearly every penny he had on the books in his vast library, and on the collection of electronic gadgets with which he surrounded himself.

There was a satellite dish on the roof that could suck in 135 television channels from outer space. The dish was connected to an elaborate video recording system and a TV screen large enough for a small movie house. The screen was connected to a high-fidelity stereo with laser disc and reel-to-reel tape. Everything was run by a computer that could do almost anything, including punch into the subscriber data base of the Smithsonian Institution.

Frankie sat on a footstool that was much too short for his long, skinny legs. He rested his elbows on knobby knees that were propped up under his chin. The speaker sat on a swivel chair with wheels.

I said, "What do you want me to do?"

The Speaker wheeled over to his computer and

punched up FRANKLIN, SIR JOHN. He said to Frankie, "What's your game, son? The paper says you're a thief and maybe a killer, but I can't say you're acting like either one—except for the snowshoes. Shoplifting is against the law. There's no doubt about it. But most criminals don't want to be on the radio, unless they're right-wing preachers looking for a cash donation."

Frankie chewed his lower lip. The Speaker peered into his computer and punched another button or two. Emily Gertevorst wheeled in a cart with a coffeepot and a tray piled high with sugar and starch. I glanced at a clock. It was just after 9:00 P.M. The northern sun was still in the sky and would be for another hour or so.

"I don't play any games, Mr. Gertevorst. I'm just trying to see that justice gets done. Here's the what's what. The time I did in the penny was because of something that lady scientist said I stole and that was a goddamn lie. They believe her because she was a professor and I'm just a surfer, but I'm just trying to get what I got coming to me. That's my right. You got to allow me that."

"I can understand that, Mr. Stubbs. But why were those three men chasing you out on the Eklunta Flats? It's a good thing they're so stupid or you'd be dead."

"I met two of those guys in the penny, when I was a crawler doing five on the phony charge I told you about. Montague, the one that's so tall—now he was a real iron man, which is what us Aussies would call a very hard case. He's got this guy what works for him that they call the Gripper. Those blokes're all in the Ned Kelly Gang."

"Is that like the Australian Mafia?" I said.

"That'd be stretching it a bit. Oz is a pretty law-abiding place, except for gambling and girls. But whatever organized crime we got, the Ned Kelly Gang is it. It's mostly thickheads and numbskulls that're too dumb to make money legal. Nothing I would worry about unless you're a guy like me. They run the penny like it's their grammy's grocery store and do a little thieving every now and then. That's what's they're up to now. They're trying to steal from me."

"But aren't you a thief?" the Speaker said.

Frankie's surfer tan turned bright red. "Absolutely not," he said. "I'm an Irish revolutionary. I have confiscated certain contraband, but only for political purposes."

The Speaker seemed intrigued by this notion, but he didn't have time to pursue it. "What're they trying to steal?" he said.

"You'll find that out if you put me on your show."

The Speaker gazed at the computer with a thoughtful look on his face. Then he rubbed his eyes with his fists, as if he was sleepy and had just had a dream. "Well, this is interesting," he announced. "Come take a look at this."

We looked over his shoulder at dark green letters on a light green screen. His computer had produced a file called SIR JOHN FRANKLIN—STUBBS INTERFACE: $15.25 PAYABLE WITHIN 30 DAYS OF INFORMATION RETRIEVAL.

"Well, what do you think of that, Mr. Stubbs? Would you pay a couple of dollars to read a title like that? I would."

Before Frankie could answer, the Speaker typed in YES. This caused the computer to start some rapid-fire printing. The Speaker removed the page from the machine, handed it to me, and said, "Read it out loud, Pres."

"Sir John Franklin—Stubbs Interface. There are two references in the available literature. One—Sir John

Franklin was lieutenant governor of the British penal colony of Tasmania from 1837 to 1843. In 1842 the Sydney Monitor *published the allegations of a female prisoner by the name of Maggie Stubbs who claimed to have borne a child fathered by Franklin in 1804. Stubbs was a known prostitute and the daughter of an Irish Catholic transported to Australia for thievery. Franklin denied the allegation and claimed it was part of a plot to discredit his administration. He blamed the Arthur Faction, a clique of established persons who opposed Franklin's liberal policies, particularly his efforts to limit the flogging of convicts. There is no evidence for the claim of Maggie Stubbs. However, it is a matter of record that Sir John Franklin visited Australia in 1803, when he was a fifteen-year-old midshipman on the* Investigator, *a British ship captained by Matthew Flinders. For original source, see the* Sydney Monitor, *June eight, 1843, page one.*

"*Two—Lady Jane Franklin was Sir John's second wife. After the controversy over Maggie Stubbs's allegations subsided, she announced her intention to form* The Tasmanian Society for the Reformation of Female Prisoners. *In remarks to the press on announcing this charity, Lady Franklin said, 'I'm very saddened by the plight of Maggie Stubbs. She has been reduced to lies and prostitution by the harsh conditions of this place, which requires a heart of stone and a frame of steel.' For original source, see the* Sydney Monitor *November nineteen, 1843, page one.*

"*This is your bill. Please pay fifteen dollars and twenty-five cents by July fourteen. The Techtel Company appreciates your patronage.*"

Frankie Stubbs looked like he'd just been kicked in the stomach. The Speaker took pity on him. "My guess is that Frankie is short for Franklin, and that you're related to Maggie Stubbs. Let me see now ... 1803 ..." He paused for a bit while he counted backward—eight fingers and a thumb. "That would be about nine generations ago, give or take a finger or two and depending on when your women have their babies. At a very early age, I would have to guess."

The Speaker and I sipped coffee while Frankie told us the legend of Maggie Stubbs, as handed down by the women in their family. I didn't believe a word of it, but here's the legend anyway.

Maggie was the daughter of Eddie Stubbs, just another Irish thief who talked like a revolutionary. Eddie'd been a flash lad in Belfast, the sort of man who has the purse of a beggar but the clothes of a gentleman. Eddie was always dancing with the cat. He kept count of every stroke of every flogging because he hoped to pay the English back some day. He'd taken 1,457 lashes in all. Eddie was a real iron man. In 1788, he was transported to the penal colony of Australia for picking a rich man's pocket or singing an Irish song, depending on whether you believe Frankie's mother or Frankie's aunt.

"Eddie was a crook with the gift of gab," Frankie's aunt would say.

"Eddie was a leader of the Irish revolution," Frankie's mother would always reply.

In Australia, Eddie danced with the cat a lot—450 lashes in Botany Bay, and 875 more in Hobart on the island of Tasmania, where the hard-core prisoners were sent. On Tasmania he worked on the road gang and impregnated a woman from the Female Factory. Eventually he bolted and was killed by the Aborigine hunters who tracked down escaped prisoners for all the rum they could drink. A few months later, Eddie's doxy gave birth to a girl and named her Maggie Stubbs.

Maggie grew up in the Female Factory, spinning good Australian wool into good English cloth. In 1801, at the age of twelve, she couldn't take it anymore and bolted into the Bush, just like her father had done. The Aborigines treated her somewhat better than the guards, although the family legend is unclear as to exactly what happened while she was in their custody. The Bushmen taught Maggie how to live on nothing, and she got as far as Kangaroo Island. There she spied the billowing canvas of the *Investigator*, a ship of the Royal Navy that anchored offshore while a mapmaker measured the coast and a scientist collected samples of the local flora and fauna. Maggie hid behind a tree until a very plump and very young midshipman by the name of John Franklin came walking by.

"Come over here, boy!" Maggie said, even though she was a year and five months younger than John.

Young John Franklin peeked behind the tree and saw that Maggie had lifted up her tattered skirt and was showing him that which he'd dreamed about night after night but had never tasted in all his fifteen years.

He tried to speak but couldn't. Maggie did all the talking. She said, "Here's the what's what, lad. You can poke it in me as long as you promise to sneak me on board your ship, and you can poke it in me again all the way to England as long as you promise to bring me some food every night. Now let's get to it before your ship sets sail."

"But Captain Flinders wouldn't approve," the midshipman said. Before he could say anything else, the pants of his uniform were crumpled around his ankles and Maggie Stubbs was doing something he hadn't even dreamed of.

Young John Franklin tried to keep his part of the bargain, but Captain Flinders found them out. He gave his midshipman a flogging and sent Maggie back to the Female Factory.

Thirty-four years later, Franklin returned to Australia. He was a lot more plump, had a lot less hair, and had had many adventures north of the Arctic Circle. He'd written books that were read by the most important people in the world. Now he was the naval governor of Tasmania, a penal colony whose criminals included Maggie Stubbs, who wasn't so young anymore. One day, Maggie stopped Sir John's carriage on the streets of Hobart and introduced the governor to Franklin Stubbs, his thirty-three-year-old bastard son.

Lady Jane Franklin was also in the carriage. Legend has it that she didn't bat an eye while Maggie was present but had a nervous breakdown when she wasn't. Lady Jane was too liberal to be angry or jealous, so she punished John and Maggie by devoting a portion of her boundless energy to improving the moral character of female prisoners. Maggie couldn't handle the shame of being saved, and died soon thereafter.

Her son, Franklin, carried on. He honored Sir John by bragging that he was his bastard son, and he honored Maggie by becoming a thief. He had a lot of children, as poor men often do, and named the oldest one after himself—Franklin Stubbs II, who also became a thief. He had a son named Franklin, who had a son named Franklin, on down to the ninth generation.

"And to hear my mum tell it, every one was a real shit, especially me. That's a family tradition too."

"So you're a thief," the Speaker said.

"We actually don't call it stealing. We always call it politics. The Stubbses used to be highly regarded until Cromwell came over to Ireland with a bunch of Protestants. They stole everything we had. They even stole the trees, if you can believe that. That's what my grandmum said. Ireland used to be covered with trees, but the English cut them all down so that they could build their navy and then go terrify somebody else. That's how come we figure it's not stealing if we steal from an Englishman. It's more like getting our own back. In the old days the Stubbses always stole horses, because only the English were rich enough to ride. I never stole anybody's horse, although I hope to do so someday."

I said, "So what do you steal then? You were in jail, right."

"I just took what belonged to me, and Bev got me arrested for it. Now she wants to dig up Sir Johnny's body and that's not right. I mean to see that he gets to rest in peace."

I didn't believe it, but the Speaker did. Or at least he wanted to believe it and decided he was going to help. The Speaker was always helping one poor soul or another. It was another way he had of repaying his family's debt to FDR, of making the New Deal seem more like a loan and less like charity.

But Frankie didn't want any help. He much preferred to complain about his troubles. The Speaker said, "That's okay. Complain all you want as long as you complain on 'Trapline.' Which starts pretty soon by the way, so you boys had best be moving along."

CHAPTER ▌▌

Frankie and I walked to the KREL trailer down a path worn smooth by the healthy hikers and teenagers in love who frequented the Bodenburg Butte. It was half-past ten and the sun was going down, but the moon was out, the sky was clear, and there was still plenty of light. I tried to shed some on Frankie Stubbs. "So what's the scam?" I said. "You're not fooling me."

But, of course, he was fooling me, and would continue to do so until long after I last saw him. For all I know, he might still be fooling me, especially when it comes to those precious sun pictures. But I'm getting ahead of myself.

Frankie said, "What're you saying, mate?"

I had the distinct impression that he was calling me "mate" because I expected him to. I said, "I'm saying that you're working on some kind of scam and I want to know what it is. I think you're nothing but an Irish thief and all that stuff about protecting frozen bodies is a typical Irish way of making crime sound noble. Like that horseshit you said about stealing from Englishmen. If you didn't bend down and kiss the Blarney Stone, then I bet the Blarney Stone jumped up and kissed you."

He pounded his forehead with his fist, as if that is how he stamped information on his brain. "Prester John Riordan's your name, right? Then you must be Irish too. Catholic Irish, of course, since the Orangemen aren't really Irish in the proper sense of the word."

I admitted that I was of Irish extraction and occasionally proud of it. The young thief then launched into a very long litany of crimes that had been committed against Irishmen. Most Irish belly-aching starts with Oliver Cromwell, and life Beyond the Pale in 1649. But Frankie went back another eight hundred years or so, to the Vikings who invaded Ireland and brought an end to the golden age of Irish monks—St. Patrick, St. Brendan, and St. Palladius, the men who bequeathed us our weepy disposition.

"See, the Irish tried learning first and that didn't work at all. We was an island full of peaceful monks and farmers and then the Vikings came. Then they tried exploring, when St. Brendan discovered America. The Sinn Fein tried politics and Sean O'Casey wrote plays. James Joyce wrote books and the IRA threw bombs and you know what, mate? None of them things worked at all. The only thing that does work is thieving because most of the English I know would rather be dead than poor. I know it sounds silly, but—"

"Hello, Frankie."

Frankie and I had been so absorbed in his diatribe

that neither of us noticed that the path to KREL had been blocked by three shadows, one of which didn't have any arms, a shadow like that which would be cast by a man wrapped in a body bandage. It was Donald Montague.

Frankie made a break for it. The two other shadows gave chase while Donald watched over me. He was at least a foot taller than I, but the bandages made him look like a larva. He said, "Don't even think about it, radio man. A cripple like you would never get away. Not from the lads what I'm working with."

This seemed to be an odd statement from a man who looked like a larva, but he was right, of course. I am a cripple and I am very slow. Even with his body bandage on he could probably run faster than I. But how could he catch me if his arms were taped tight?

I ran too, although it wasn't really a run. It was more of a shuffle-shuffle-skip. Donald gave chase but stumbled on a root and dropped facedown like a bag of groceries, his head being a melon of sorts.

"Hey, Gripper!" he screamed. "Get over here and stand me up. I'm going to stomp on that bastard's face."

I headed back to the Speaker's house but was run to the ground before I'd taken ten skips. It was the man with bad teeth whom I'd seen in court. I smelled tobacco and unwashed leather as he dragged me by the hair to where Donald had fallen down.

Donald had managed to roll onto his back. His face was a mess of leaves glued on with blood. "You're a dead man," he said to me. "I'm going to step on your face as soon as I get my arms." He turned to the Gripper and said, "Where's Frankie?"

The Gripper let go of my hair and helped Donald to

his feet. "The pilot'll chase him down," he said. The Gripper was Australian too. "You know how fast he is."

Donald nodded and stuck out his jaw, which seemed to say, "Of course, the pilot'll get him. What was I thinking of?" Then he looked at me and said to the Gripper, "I want you to hold him down so I can step on his face."

The Gripper turned away, pretending he didn't hear. Donald pressed the point, so his partner said, "This isn't the place, Donnie. We'll go back to the motor home and if you want I'll hold his legs apart so's you can kick him in the balls. How about that? Would that make you happy?"

We inched down a path that ran down the southern slope of the Bodenburg Butte. The Gripper kept one hand on Donald's collar, so he wouldn't stumble, and the other on my hair, so I wouldn't run away. It was a very long and painful trip down to the Old Glenn Highway, and a large motor home parked behind the cemetery. We made ourselves comfortable in the motor home and sat down to wait for Frankie and the pilot.

Donald and the Gripper played a card game in the kitchen area of the motor home, a plush Winnebago with miniature versions of all the usual conveniences. I had to hold Donald's cards. He pointed at his play with his nose. I tried to make conversation, but they didn't want to talk.

I said, "So, Don, how are you feeling? When do they take the bandages off?"

Donald ignored me and pointed his nose at a ten of clubs. I played it on the Gripper's jack of spades. The card game they were playing was called Sheepshead and it made no sense at all. The order of the cards was all confused. Queens were stronger than kings and tens were worth more than jacks.

I said, "I don't know what the problem is, but you should probably know that I'm supposed to be on the radio now and people are going to notice that I'm not."

This was a lie. "Trapline" was canceled on a fairly regular basis, when a guest didn't show or I went on vacation. The Kountry Klassics Komputer filled in the time with Randy Travis and Emmie Lou Harris and nobody complained too much.

"I'll crack you," the Gripper said. This had something to do with the game. It meant he was doubling the bet. Donald could fold, crack back, or play a card. He told the Gripper to turn on the radio. We listened to KREL Kountry Radio. The San Antonio deejays hadn't missed a beat in my absence. Waylon Jennings sang a song of cowboy love. The Speaker might notice that I wasn't on the air, but no one else would.

Donnie said, "I don't hear where they've got an 'all alert' out on you."

Cowboys sang songs about whiskey and women to the lonely twang of their sad guitars. Frankie and the pilot showed up shortly after 4:00 A.M. The sun was already up, but the butte was still asleep and would remain so for two more hours.

The pilot was a Canadian. He said, "I found the little hoser hiding in a barn about five hundred meters from the radio shack. I would have been quicker but I had to be quiet. There was a house nearby."

That would be the Speaker's house. He wouldn't have noticed a ruckus by the barn. He would have thought it just some more teenagers in love. In the summer months they climbed up onto the butte to look at the stars and do that which teenage couples do. The Speaker never disturbed them. The Matanuska Valley was a farming community, and he was a tolerant man.

CHAPTER 12

The Canadian was lean and melancholy, like an aging hockey player saddened by the knowledge that his glory days were over, that he'd gone from chasing pucks on ice to chasing Australians in the weeds. Long limbs protruded from hiking shorts and a Hawaiian shirt. He'd made some efforts to compensate for the fact that he was going bald: woolly sideburns framed his face, and the few remaining hairs on top were curled around the crown of his head in the general shape of a very loose spring. He drove the Winnebago as if it were built for speed instead of comfort, motoring fast down the straightaways, cutting corners and working the brakes.

"Take it easy on the curves," Donald said. "The blues'll be on us if you tip her over." Donald would have tipped over on every curve if the Gripper hadn't steadied him with a hand on the scruff of his neck. His other hand held a gun, which he pointed at Frankie and me every now and then.

After we'd driven for a mile or two, Donald told the Canadian to park the Winnebago at the next turnoff. When this was done he had the Gripper unfasten his seat belt so he could turn around and look Frankie in the eye without sliding onto the floor.

He said, "I think it's time we should go about our business. I want to take a look at the goods, Frankie. If you give us any trouble, the Gripper is going to blow your brains out right here and now. You remember Grip when we was in the penny. He's the one what kicked your arse for not cooperating. You're still not cooperating, and it's starting to get on my nerves."

Frankie made a noncommittal grunt. Donald turned to his companion. "Use the knife, Grip. The gun'll make too much noise and the blues'll be after us."

Frankie stalled for as long as it took the Gripper to produce a large hunting knife and wave it under his chin. Frankie said, "Step back a bit, will you, sport, and I'll get the goods right now."

On a signal from Donald, the Gripper backed away. He kept his knife at the ready as Frankie dug into his pants and removed a thin plastic envelope that hadn't prevented the letter within from turning yellow and crumbling to dust at the edges.

"Another family tradition," Frankie said to me. "It was mostly just a keepsake that was always given to the oldest girl as a way of saying that the Stubbses were more than just shanty Irish trash. It never meant anything more than that. But now that they've got this Vibroseise Device, it could mean a lot if they ever find anything."

Donald told him to read the following letter:

* * *

THE FROZEN FRANKLIN

London, England
May 18, 1845

My dearest Maggie Stubbs,

You cannot imagine the turmoil that has af-
flicted my life since you stopped us on the street
and introduced me to my only son. Sometimes I
am about to drown in the guilt I feel over the pain
caused by the youthful indiscretion we enjoyed
behind the bushes on Kangaroo Island. At other
times, I must confess that I am overcome with joy
at the thought that I finally have a son. My first
marriage produced but a daughter, and I have
now concluded that my union with Lady Jane will
bear no fruit.

I can do nothing to compensate for the thirty-
seven years of suffering and privation you and my
son, Franklin, have borne. I can, however, do
something to improve your situation in the future.

I will soon be leaving England on a Voyage of
Discovery through the Northwest Passage. The
successful completion of the mission will deliver
me to the Pacific Ocean. At that juncture, I will
then proceed to Australia, where I hope to join
with you and young Franklin. With me I will
bring certain items which may secure your future
and that of our son. It is my fervent hope that this
will in some way compensate you for these many
years of neglect.

Sincerely,
J. Franklin

"I don't believe it," the Gripper said after Frankie
had finished reading the letter. I also believed the
letter to be a forgery but that's beside the point
because no one asked for my opinion. In any case, this

was a forgery made real by the fact that so many Australians believed it to be authentic. Donald, for one, thought the letter was worth stealing. He had the Gripper fold it carefully into its plastic envelope and tuck it into a crease in his body bandage. Then he turned to Frankie and said, "Now we talk some business. Ned Kelly gets the customary fifty percent. How we split the rest is up to you and me."

They negotiated quite some time over who would get how much of what. The "who" were Frankie, Donald, the Gripper, and the Ned Kelly Gang. The "how much" was calculated according to a formula that started with the gang (50 percent) and ended with the Gripper (5 percent). Frankie and Donald would split the rest and neither seemed to like it much.

Frankie said, "The goods belong to me by rights. I should get a bigger cut."

Donald said, "But I've got all the expenses. Paying the pilot and renting the plane. Purchasing all the provisions. Then there's the matter of hospital bills. Two blokes're dead, and I got my arms taped up. Those things all cost money and it's your fault it happened. I should step on your face for almost killing me."

"My fault! It's your fault. I didn't know you were following me. That's what you get for sneaking around in the dark like that."

Donald squirmed a bit, as if he wanted to make a gesture, but forgot that his arms were taped to his body. "The best thing is for both of us to say we was both in the wrong and talk about something else. Let's talk about these goods we're looking for. What are we looking for anyway?"

Frankie didn't know. "The eggheads'll handle that.

They've got this new kind of machine they call the Vibroseise Device. It pounds the ground and listens for sound. I'm not sure how it works. It's never been used like this before, to look for some goodies in the snow. But if they find anything that belonged to Sir Johnny, then I'm going to say it's mine."

Donald said, "Not mine. Ours. And Ned Kelly gets his fifty percent."

"I bet it's a sheep ranch," the Gripper said. "The gang will be very disappointed if we go to all this trouble for a silly flock of sheep."

"I think it is a gold mine," Frankie replied. "Sir Johnny spent some time near Kalgoorlie. There's lots of gold up there. That's why they call it the Golden Mile. I think we're going to be rich."

I'd heard about convicts and the thousand-yard stare, but I'd never seen one before. Now I saw three of them, as the criminals each gazed at their own personal visions of the untold riches of Oz. The Canadian was amused. He could afford to be, since he got paid by the hour and the mile and didn't have to worry about the eventual profits of the enterprise.

When they were done talking business, Donald Montague said, "We need to dump this stiff someplace."

I looked at Donald. Everyone else looked at me. I said, "What stiff?" The Gripper made a snorting sound.

Frankie said, "I wouldn't dump him yet. He's got some juice with the lady scientist. That's why I was going to be on his radio show, to find out how much he knows about things. But you had to go and bollix it all up."

Donald became so excited that he lost his balance

and tipped over onto his face. Frankie enjoyed a laugh. The Gripper stifled one. The Canadian leaned over and lifted his employer back into his seat.

The Australians decided to test the claim that I had juice with the lady scientist. I wanted to have some juice with her, because it was important to my captors and kept Donald from stepping on me. I wasn't quite certain what juice was, but I prayed to God that I might have some. I later learned that "juice" is Australian slang for buckets of come and means power of any sort and the sense to know how to use it. Australians, whether they be thieves, kidnappers, or scientists, use lots of peculiar slang. After my ordeal was over, I talked to an Australian friend about some of the words they used. His name is Gareth and he drives a delivery truck for the *Matanuska News-Nugget*. Here is a glossary, according to Gareth, of unique words and phrases that Australian people use:

1) *The big smoke:* A large city like Sydney or Melbourne
2) *Bonzer:* Beautiful, fantastic
3) *Blues:* The police and other armed authorities
4) *To be crook:* To be ill or sick, as in Rookwood, a famous cemetery near Sydney
5) *Donger:* The beef bayonet, or mulligan, or tummy banana, or pencil, or the Malone, or the unemployed; the male member
6) *Norks:* Lots of fun
7) *Oz:* Australia
8) *Pat Malone:* To be alone with one's beef bayonet
9) *Quantas hostie:* A beautiful woman.

10) *Wizards of Oz:* Judges, jailers, and other
    important public officials

For some reason that I still don't completely understand, they have dozens of colorful ways of saying "to
pee" and "to fornicate." More information on this
will be provided later on.

Donald said to me, "Okay, Mr. Radio Star. Here's
the what's what. You're going to talk to the Quantas
hostie and the Gripper'll be there too. They say he's
got the strongest hands in Oz, from always waxing his
oar. If you screw up he'll break your neck right then
and there. Remember that and you'll be all right."

The staging area for the Franklin Recovery Expedition was an old Colony Barn on the Experimental
Farm. Dr. Bud was allowing them to use the facility
free of charge, all in the name of science. He enter-
tained the delusion that he might get his face on
"Science Today," a weekly show on National Public
TV. He believed that such a scientific coup would
make up for a lifetime of imperfect seed potatoes.

The X-Farm seemed like an unlikely location for a
"Science Today" shoot. The barn was dark and
stacked to the rafters with disassembled farm imple-
ments: a rusty combine, a milking machine, and the
wheels of a faulty tractor. The fields outside were
visually uninspiring, as they were mostly planted with
row upon row of experimental plants and a few
enormous vegetables, which aren't nearly as interesting as they sound. A certain cabbage had caught the
attention of the TV crew. The photographer and
sound man pointed their instruments at the leafy
sprout while seven other people with notebooks and
clipboards supervised their work.

Dr. Godwin was standing next to an experimental cow behind the Colony Barn. The poor beast had a tube sticking out of its belly so that the scientists could peek inside and see how she was digesting her food. The cow mooed when she saw me and the Gripper, and ignored us after deciding that we weren't going to look at her cud.

"Afternoon, Mr. Riordan," Dr. Godwin said.

I introduced her to the Gripper, whom I identified as an Australian TV journalist, an old news crony of mine. She nodded and mumbled something polite. He flashed her a purple smile full of gingivitis.

"I'm just checking up on you," I said. "You seemed pretty upset after the 'Trapline' show. That guy who called from prison said some pretty harsh things to you."

She turned away and looked at the cow. The scientist had a nicely shaped butt, kept trim, I decided, by the heavy work of digging up corpses frozen in the permafrost. Without looking back she said, "Lots of blokes have said lots of things to me. I don't pay much attention to men. Forget about it, all right?"

Since she wasn't looking at us, the Gripper was able to make all sorts of hand signals, none of which made any sense to me. I said, "Now tell me again where you're going?"

Again without looking back she replied, "It's called King William Island. It's a big frozen rock with a few Eskimos on it. The Eskimos remember Captain Crozier in their legends, and I'm hoping they'll give us some kind of clue about where we should start taking soundings with the Vibroseise Device. My guess is we should go north. That's where Captain Crozier's body would be, unless they fed him to the dogs, in which case his body isn't anyplace and 'Science Today' will be quite disappointed."

The Gripper said, "What's a Vibroseise Device?"

"It's a big sort of jackhammer thing. The Yank oil companies use it to locate petrochemicals. It shakes up the ground like a little earthquake and then listens to sound waves in the permafrost. We're looking for bones and silverware. Silverware makes one kind of sound. Frozen bones make another. Either one should help us along if we look in the proper place. North, I say. Everyone's looked in the south already, but I figure Captain Crozier went north, hoping he'd get picked up by a Scottish whaling ship."

I remembered those tears she'd shed on my late night radio show. I'd never seen an Ice Queen melt before. I wanted to tell her the truth, but a mind picture kept getting in the way. In it we were lying together in a field of enormous vegetables. My throat was cut, her neck was broken, and the Gripper was laughing at us.

The Gripper made a signal I didn't understand. I remembered what Donald had told me to say. "Just what do you think you're going to find? Besides all those frozen stiffs, I mean."

This time she turned around and looked me right in the eyes. She wasn't surprised. Only disappointed. It must have been another Ice Queen who'd cried. "I see where you've been talking to Frankie," she said. "Frankie's a liar and a thief. My advice is don't believe him, and if you're talking to him you won't be talking to me. So just bugger off, all right."

Dr. Bud intercepted the Gripper and me as we headed for the X-Farm parking lot. My friend was carrying a bag full of something that could have been seed potatoes. He was in a state of great excitement.

"It's a done deal, Pres. The colonel says we can use the Herc and I'll be the guy that flies it. It's good PR for the National Guard. We've got to do something useful if the Cold War is really over."

I wanted to move on. The Gripper wanted to stay. I saw another mind picture. This time my neck was broken and Dr. Bud's throat was cut. I introduced the Gripper to my friend. Dr. Bud had never met an Australian journalist before.

"This'll be quite a show," he said. "First 'Science Today' and now you. We scientists love to be famous. That way we're able to do less work for more money."

"What are they looking for, Bud? Besides government grants, I mean."

The scientist shook his head, as if boggled by the magnitude of the question I had asked. "Everybody's looking for different things. I'll be flying a Herc full of brains. It's a holiday for eggheads. There's a botanist who writes about desert plants. Now he'll be collecting tundra. And then there's a young mammalian biologist who's very interested in predators. He wants to do a paper on the walrus and the polar bear. There's a geologist and several naval historians . . ."

And several criminals, I wanted to add but didn't, because I saw another one of those discouraging mind pictures. In this one Dr. Bud's neck was broken and my throat was cut.

Bud continued: ". . . a toxicologist who wants to test this theory the Canadians have that they all caught a bit of lead poisoning. Then there's Beverly Godwin, of course. She's collecting Eskimo legends but you already know about her. There's also a very peculiar fellow who calls himself a photogrammarian."

Even the Gripper caught that one. "What's that?" he said.

"He can look at a photograph and tell you where it was taken, and when, by examining the shadows and making some calculations. He'll be looking for 'sun pictures,' an early kind of photograph that Sir John Franklin may have snapped."

He paused for a moment, then continued. "Or maybe not. This is a bit of a lark and a bit of a fishing expedition. Maybe they'll catch a whopper and maybe they won't catch anything. It's hard to say for sure until you start digging, right, Mr. Waldrop?"

That's how I'd introduced the Gripper, as Peter Waldrop, TV journalist. Bud smiled and offered him an imperfect seed potato.

The Canadian pilot had parked the Winnebago on the quiet side of the Bodenburg Butte, away from the motorized hustle and bustle caused by the Old Glenn Highway.

"Frankie is full of horseshit," the Gripper reported to Donald as soon as we were settled in. "The man doesn't have any juice with the lady scientist. She wouldn't even give him the time of day. She didn't even turn around when he was talking to her. She kept looking at this silly cow with a tube sticking out of its belly. Funny as a bagful of arseholes, as far as I'm concerned."

Donald paced the length of the Winnebago. It didn't take him very long. He came to a stop in front of me. He looked comic in his bandages, but I didn't laugh.

"When did she say they're leaving?"

"Tomorrow sometime," I said. "She didn't say

exactly when. They're going to a place called King William Island. I've never heard of it before. Anyway, they've got the Herc and a pilot to fly it, but they've still got a lot of packing to do." Then I added, as an afterthought, "Then there's the Vibroseise Device. The Gripper forgot to tell you about that."

Donald looked at the Gripper, who shrugged his shoulders and looked away. I could tell by the look in the Gripper's eyes that he was starting to hate me.

"What the hell is this Vibroseise thing? What is it supposed to do?"

I pretended to know a lot more than I did, and testified to several imaginary details. Donald seemed convinced and decided not to step on me just yet, until he was certain I'd outlived my usefulness.

CHAPTER 13

The Canadian pilot glided the Winnebago into a parking lot across the road from the Matanuska armory of the Alaska National Guard. Our stakeout was disguised by the presence of three other recreational vehicles—two more Winnies and a Cruiser King with its own satellite dish on top.

The occupants of the other RVs were all white and mostly older. They milled about the parking lot and seemed to know each other, as if they'd just arrived by caravan from Meadowbrook Hills, Ohio. Four women played dominoes in lawn furniture arranged around a portable picnic table. The flicker of a tiny color TV made it look like an outdoor version of somebody's living room.

"Gudday," the Gripper said to the tourists as he stepped down from our Winnie with a portable grill and an armload of steaks. "Hope you don't mind us camping here, but this is the best spot in town." The ladies who were playing dominoes murmured their approval, so he started heating up the barbie. His job was to make dinner and act normal while Donald and the pilot spied on the gathering of Australian scientists.

The Matanuska armory of the Alaska National Guard is located at the intersection of Bogard and Seward Meridian, two of the most unfortunate roads in the valley. Bogard winds around hills and trees like a snake that has lost its way. Seward Meridian is a death trap constructed by the borough assembly for no apparent purpose. Its main function is to provide speeding teens with a shortcut to the liquor store.

The armory is located in the empty belly of an enormous gravel pit. Tanks, trucks, and planes, all painted camouflage green, wait in silence for freedom-hating Communists to come pouring across the Bering Strait. Next door is the reinforced concrete bunker used by the Alaska Division of Emergency Services, formerly known as Civil Defense. Like their next-door neighbors, the people who work there are waiting, with decreasing certainty, for somebody to do something crazy. Their supervisor is a cigar-chomping Democrat with long-standing personal ties to the Gertevorst family and other important people.

And finally, across the gravel driveway, in the middle of an attractive lawn manicured by indolent llamas, is the Tsunami Warning Center. It is a listening post for scientists who monitor earthquakes from around the world.

The location of these three institutions in the same gravel pit is not a coincidence. When the Conover family finished scraping the gravel away, solid bedrock remained. The geologists at the Tsunami Warning Center had measured it and pronounced it 1.13

miles thick, making it one of the hardest places on Earth. Because it was also off the beaten track, it was the perfect place for agencies that only become important when horrible things happen. Quakes couldn't move it and bombs couldn't melt it. I still didn't feel very safe.

"What's going on?" Frankie said.

The two of us shared a single window and took turns looking out of it. "Just a bunch of smart people looking at a plane. There's Dr. Godwin. You remember her."

Frankie nudged me aside and poked his nose through the curtains. The person who'd decorated the Winnie was partial to grease-stained polka-dots and had given the vehicle a cute name: The Road Worrier. I assume the Winnie had been stolen by the Australian thieves.

We could see Dr. Bud supervise the loading of an astounding array of technology into the cargo plane: TV cameras, several all-terrain vehicles, and the Vibroseise Device. There were piles and piles of boxes and boxes full of strange and marvelous things that only a scientist could appreciate. There were also more mundane supplies: food, water, and extra clothing; lots of boots and extra mittens. The expedition was well-prepared for something. I did not ask what for, but feared for the worst in the absence of more information.

A great commotion was made over the Vibroseise Device. Dr. Godwin petted it. Dr. Bud made sure it was secure and the guys from the Tsunami Warning Center admired it from afar. They turned it on for a little while to make sure it was working. A pipe belched thick black diesel smoke and the pile driver struck the ground with a rapid series of powerful blows. It made a big noise and produced a steady vibration that traveled through the bedrock, across the road, over the parking lot, into the Winnie, and up my legs. An Australian listened through a pair of headphones and nodded in a meaningful way. The television crew rolled some tape for "Science Today."

"What're they doing?" Donald asked.

I explained the device as best as I could. Donald didn't understand. Frankie didn't believe me. The Canadian pilot didn't say a word. He seemed to be thinking about something that had nothing to do with science, crime, or subsurface turbulence.

We wolfed down the overcooked steaks and took turns watching the scientists. A modest fuss was created when their plane taxied onto the runway in the late afternoon. The Speaker stopped by to say a few words and the Palmer Junior High School Band played their version of "Waltzing Matilda." Dr. Godwin waved good-bye to the Speaker and Dr. Bud took the Herc down the runway and up into the sky. The Herc waved with its big green wings as it climbed out of the gravel pit and took a long, slow turn before heading north and east, in the general direction of nowhere.

The Canadian pilot said, "We can go right now or we can wait all day if you want. The longer we wait the farther ahead they're going to get. It doesn't matter to me. I get paid by the hour and the mile."

The Palmer City Airport was more like a potato field that was putting on airs. Only the runway was paved. The rest of the field—sixty-five acres on the outskirts of town—was mostly graded gravel with a little dirt mixed in. Weeds cropped up except in the narrow paths frequented by cars, people, and planes.

"Here's your choices, eh?" the Canadian pilot said. "It comes down to speed or size. If we load up now, it'll slow you down. If you want to get there as quick as we can, we've got to travel light."

I wanted to carry plenty of cargo, but nobody asked me.

The pilot said, "The problem is that the Herc's got both speed and size, eh? We've got to move fast if we want to keep up."

"I don't want to spend a lot of money," Donald said, "but we need to get there fast. We better travel light, and buy some supplies on the way."

The Canadian pilot's plane was parked at the far end of a long row. It was a small commuter model with a decal on the wing—log letters in a circle that read: ARCTIC ADVENTURE, INC. Half of the passengers' seats had been removed. The interior of the fuselage was stained brown with the blood of a thousand kills. There were five men and three seats. The Gripper and I sat on the floor.

"What'll we do for food?" the Gripper said to Donald.

Donald was strapped tightly into the copilot's seat, so there'd be no danger of his tipping over. He thought about the question but didn't answer it. Instead, he ignored it, hoping it would go away.

We climbed to 3,500 feet and headed over the Talkeetna Mountains in a NNE direction. For a while we traveled parallel to the course of the Matanuska River. We could look down and see it collect water from smaller streams and squeeze it into rapids where the mountains pressed against each other. The soft shadows made by clouds glided over the birch and spruce trees that thrive in places that men leave alone.

The plane buzzed a lonely solo until the Canadian pilot announced that we were about to pass over the Trans-Alaska Pipeline.

"The pipeline has a pump station at a town coming up that they call Glennallen. We'll land there to get some fuel and then we'll make straight for the Yukon border. The Gripper'll have to keep a pretty close eye on the Radio Star."

The Glennallen airport was right next to Pump Station #11, a collection of powerful machinery that propelled the oil up the north side of the Chugach Mountains so it could slide down south to Valdez.

The Gripper kept us pinned in the back of the plane and Donald remained fastened to his seat while the Canadian supervised the refueling of the plane. The odor of the bloodstained floor was stronger now that the plane was not ventilated by motion. I wanted to gag but dare not. Frankie and the Gripper didn't seem to notice, as if they'd been smelling blood for years.

After we were airborne again, we passed around a bag of food the Canadian had purchased at the airport store. All major food groups were represented— mixed party nuts, beef jerky, potato chips, and V-8 vegetable juice cocktail. Dairy products were represented by a bag of stale Cheetos. Donald couldn't feed himself so the Gripper tossed some party nuts into his mouth. Frankie hunched over a stick of beef jerky.

"What's next?" Donald asked the Canadian.

"What do you mean?" the Canadian said.

"I mean what's the next stop and how long is it until we get there? I'm tired of sitting strapped in this bloody airplane, and I do mean bloody, right. It smells like the slaughterhouse in Cloncurry."

"We can fly straight and make the Yukon tonight if you can stand to sit there for another six hours. Then we can refuel in Dawson City and catch up on some sleep. First thing tomorrow we'll cut your bandage off and see how your arms're doing. There's sure to be a doctor in Dawson if we have to wrap you up again."

CHAPTER 14

I'd been to Canada once before, when I was six years old. There's a shrine in Montreal. I forget the name exactly. Our Lady of the Canucks, or something to that effect. It wasn't Lourdes or Fatima, but it was within driving distance of Chicago. We stood in a long line to kiss the Our Lady's toe and purchase some official Our Lady of the Canucks holy water. The holy water stand was next to a room full of discarded crutches and wheelchairs that were mounted on the wall like bowling trophies. My mother rubbed some of the holy water on my polio leg and prayed as hard as she could. She became very annoyed with me because I didn't think it was going to work. It didn't work, so we went home. That's how I spent my Canadian vacation. The next summer we went to Hot Springs, Georgia, where FDR took the cure when he was the president. That didn't work any better, but it was a lot more fun.

Still, Montreal was a wonderful place, with great

tall buildings, a river in the middle, and lots of people speaking French and acting almost as badly. Dawson City, on the other hand, was a typical Canadian dump. One street was lined with taverns, the other with overpriced motels. The place where the two streets intersected had a gas station on each corner. Population 881.

Dawson City used to be an exciting place if the stories they tell are true. It was built in a hurry during the Klondike Gold Rush of 1898. That was probably the last hurry Dawson has seen. The people try to keep up appearances, with a hitching post or two, taverns with saloonlike gates, and lots of overweight men in beards, but that's all for show. These days, Dawson City is mostly a lonely island of noise surrounded by thousands of square miles of quiet.

We camped in a field near where the Klondike River empties into the Yukon. The Gripper went into town for some beer, which he referred to with great affection as "foaming frosties." The Canadian pilot, meanwhile, used a dip net to catch us a big bucket full of Klondike grayling. He talked about Dawson City while gutting the grayling with a razor-sharp trench knife.

"The gold comes down from MacKenzie Mountains and settles in the creeks around here. The first strike was in 1896 by a man named Carmack who married an Indian woman. They named a city after him someplace over there, but nobody lives there now, eh?"

He pointed at some emptiness with the business end of his trench knife, then brought it down hard on the head of a grayling. The head popped off like a champagne cork. "They loaded a full ton of gold on the steamship *Portland* and it caused quite a ruckus when it landed in Seattle. A year after that there were forty-five thousand hosers living here, digging in the creeks and making a mess of things. Most of them never found any gold, because Carmack and the other old-timers had already staked out all the good claims."

We drank the beer, ate the fish, and talked about the gold. The general consensus among the Australians was that there must be easier ways to make a dollar or a pound and all of them had to do with stealing. As the foaming frosties were consumed, the Australians started to play an elaborate drinking game which required that each and every urination be announced in poetic metaphor. Even Frankie joined in the fun.

Donald "strained the potatoes," Frankie "drained the dragon," and the Gripper "shook hands with the unemployed." The Canadian pilot and I kept our mouths shut and our zippers zipped.

The idea of the game was to produce the most piss and poetry. Donald "watered the horses" and Frankie "wrestled with the rattlesnake." The Gripper was "pointing percy" when a man drove by our camp in a Plymouth with a red light on top and the seal of the Royal Canadian Mounted Police emblazoned on the side.

"What's going on here, eh? There's an outhouse over by the airport. If you hosers don't use it you'll find yourself taking your next leak in the Dawson City jail. Every cell's got a potty, so you won't never be more than ten feet away."

The Mountie sat up straight, squared his shoulders behind the wheel. He wore a peaked hat with a flat brim and practiced a penetrating stare. All in all, he looked like he belonged on a horse. Driving very slowly, he continued on his rounds. The Australians toasted him with foaming frosties while cursing him with whispers.

The Gripper said, "Back in the penny I once shared a cell with this crawler from Canada. He said the Mounties always get their man. He said it might not be the man what did it, but they always get somebody."

Donald was wedged between the Gripper and a tree so he wouldn't fall down. He said, "I got arrested by the Mounties once, when I was a sailor in the Royal Navy. They cuffed me for stealing in Vancouver while I was out on shore leave. They let me go after I promised I wouldn't come back. I guess I lied about that."

Later, after the air was cooler and the foaming frosties were warmer, the pilot brought out a brightly colored map of northern Canada. The lakes were blue, the mountains brown, and the valleys different shades of green. North of the Arctic Circle, the colors were whitewashed with snow. He pointed at a lonely island in a frozen sea. Red letters identified it as King William Island. It had a single black dot along its southern shore. The village was named Gjoa Havn after who knows what.

"I would guess that the trappers go there to sell their furs and buy supplies. We'll need a load of lettuce if that's where we go to get our food and camping gear."

"Well, we don't have a load of lettuce," Donald Montague replied. "I'm working with a very tight purse, and most of my money is going to you."

I thought I heard the Gripper groan, although I wasn't sure if he was groaning about the tightness of Donald's purse or the location of King William Island.

King William Island was a not-quite-square peg in a

not-so-round hole. It looked like a cardboard box that had gotten wet and listed to the left. To the south was mainland Canada, and a place called Starvation Cove. To the north and west were more frozen islands, to the east a peninsula jutted north from the mainland. These land masses forced the sea around the island into four large straits and channels that formed an X-shaped intersection.

"We'll make for Gjoa Havn," the pilot said. "There should be food and shelter there, and a place to refuel the plane."

Donald nodded. Frankie said, "How far ahead are they now would you say?"

The pilot did a quick calculation. "By now they'll be at Fort Franklin for sure. Maybe to the Coppermine River if they're in a big hurry and didn't take a rest stop."

We looked at the map, searching for these places. Donald said, "They probably stopped, I'm sure. So what about this Gjoa Havn? How much money are we talking about?"

The pilot made another calculation. "Food and shelter are real expensive in a nowhere place like that, and airplane fuel is out of sight. If the Eskimos are smart, and you can bet they are, they'll charge us for drinking water too. The scientists are going to be buying lots of stuff, so that'll jack up the price. We might as well go back to Alaska if you don't have ten thousand dollars American—not counting my fee, of course."

"Let's get to it," Donald said. "But first we take off these bandages. My arms feel like they're never going to move again."

"Don't do it, Donnie," the Gripper said. "You remember what the doctor said."

The doctor had told him to wear the bandages for at least a month. The month still had three weeks to go, but Donald couldn't wait anymore. "Cut them off now," he said. "Or I'll have to step on your face."

The Gripper cut the bandage and unwrapped his partner. His hands were tucked under his elbows and tied into a clinging embrace with a short green strap. The Gripper cut the strap off and the embrace relaxed a bit. Donald made a noise that seemed to express both pain and relief, as if he were being whipped and enjoying every stroke. It took him a while to escape from his own embrace, but every little move seemed to hurt a little better. When his hands were down at his sides, he turned to Frankie and said, "You shouldn't have done that, Frankie—lead us out on the mud like that."

"Well, you shouldn't've been chasing me. I'm not a part of the Ned Kelly Gang."

"That's not so," Donald replied. "Ned Kelly says you are."

They argued about old times until the sun went down, which happens just after midnight during midsummer in Dawson City. I shared a tent with Frankie, and he told me about Donald and the Gripper, and life in Syd's Penny, the Sydney Institute for the Reformation of Felonious Males.

Donald and Frankie had been cellmates in Northie, the north block of Syd's Penny. Frankie was doing time for theft, Donald for extortion and assault. They talked to each other a lot, because there was nothing else to do and no one else to talk to. Frankie told Donald a lot of lies, about fortunes he'd made and women he'd had. One day, when he was too tired to think up a story, he decided to tell him the truth, that he was the many times great-grandson of Sir John Franklin and Maggie Stubbs.

Frankie's whisper filled the tent. "That was my big mistake, sport, because later I find out that Donald and the Gripper are hooked up with the Ned Kelly Gang. I knew I was in trouble, and haven't had a moment's peace since then."

"What's the Ned Kelly Gang?" I said.

Frankie told me that I didn't want to know. "Stay dumb and you might be okay. They'll kill you if they think that you know too much. The Ned Kelly Gang keeps a low profile, and you've got that radio show. They don't want to be on the radio. You can bet money on that."

Donald's condition was much improved in the morning. He was able to straighten his arms, bend down and touch his toes without so much as a wimper. He threw punches at the air, short jabs with long arms. His hands were as big as steam shovels and looked like a deadly blur. "Gimme a target," he said.

He was speaking to the Gripper. The Gripper looked at me. "Why don't you step on the Radio Star. You've been talking about it for two days now. We don't need him anyway."

I tried to get away but didn't get very far. It's hard to run with a polio leg. The Gripper held my arms and spun me around as Donald circled to my left. He flicked the tip of my nose with a series of lightning blows—hooks, jabs, and haymakers. Most of the blows felt like a fly had landed. The last one felt like a railroad train and caused my nose to explode with blood.

"Sorry about that, sport. I must be getting tired, right? I'll stop for now, but we'll try again later. I appreciate your help."

The Gripper released my arms. The Canadian pilot handed me a rag. I held it to my nose until the bleeding stopped.

Our next stop was Fort Franklin, the gateway to the Franklin Mountains. These were the first geographical clues that we were approaching our destination. The Canadian pilot pulled out his map of the Northwest Territories. The Australians passed it around until it got to Frankie, who wouldn't let go.

Most of that part of the world was named by or after English explorers of the nineteenth century. They named King William Island after an English king and Victoria Island after a queen. They named Cambridge Bay after an English university, Melville Sound after a viscount, and Albert Sound after a prince.

Sir John Franklin's tragic death led to another round of nomenclature. There's Franklin Island, Franklin Strait, Cape Franklin, Franklin Lake, and Point Franklin. Then there's Lady Franklin Point, Lady Franklin Bay, Cape Jane Franklin, and Cape Lady Franklin. One of the three Northwest Territories is called the District of Franklin. It is almost as big as Alaska and very much colder. It is made up of ice, sea, and permafrost, has 5,476 people and no trees. It is the last place on earth for everything but ice, snow, and polar bears.

Fort Franklin was situated on the southeast corner of the Great Bear Lake, about one hundred miles from the Arctic Circle and seven hundred miles from our destination. It had a runway, a few mobile homes, and a store. The store was located in what used to be the fort, a square building made of logs. In front of the store was a bronze statue of the great explorer, weathered by the elements and very proud of it.

Donald checked out prices in the store while the Canadian pilot refueled his plane. The Gripper purchased some foaming frosties and promised to piss them all away. Frankie and I looked at the statue and read the inscription beneath it:

SIR JOHN FRANKLIN—THE POLAR KNIGHT
1786 to 1847

> He fought with Nelson at Trafalgar,
> And helped lose the battle of New Orleans.
> He walked to the Polar Sea and back,
> With a hungry band of brave Marines.
> After that Australia with Lady Jane, his wife.
> After that the Northwest Passage,
> Which cost Sir John his life.

Frankie studied the inscription for quite some time, as if trying to memorize it. He was a son in search of a father that he'd read about but never seen. How would the real man stack up against the man he'd imagined all these years? Not well, perhaps; but he kept looking anyway.

"Sir John should go on a diet," I said.

The sculptor had made no attempt to give the Polar Knight a heroic figure. Bald and full of jowl, he looked like a maker of fine pastries who'd eaten too much of his own rich stock.

Frankie said, "I'll never figure it out. Everybody

else starved to death and he had a heart attack. I'd be ashamed to have a heart attack if I was a guy like him."

I bit my tongue but said it anyway. "Maybe you are a guy like him and don't even know it yet."

CHAPTER 15

The days stopped having nights. The land stopped having landmarks. The world north of Fort Franklin was flat and cold. Any features it may have possessed had been obliterated by shifting masses of ice and snow.

We flew along the channel of Back's Great Fish River until it spilled into the polar sea in the general vicinity of the place where mainland Canada comes close to the south shore of King William Island. The sea between the island and the mainland heaved and shifted like a great Ice Monster waking up from its winter sleep. Huge icebergs clogged the narrow channel, their proud, irregular shapes floating along with the current like sailing ships made of snow. They jostled one another and sometimes collided, sending chunks of blue ice bigger than small buildings splashing into the sea. The smaller chunks of ice made by these collisions continued to float in a determined way, as if they were tired of their arctic eternity and wanted a meltdown to set them free.

"Some of those icebergs're a hundred thousand years old, as old as the first Ice Age," the Canadian pilot said. "They're melting now, eh, if you can believe that. Some say it's the Greenhouse effect. I think that's a bunch of horseshit, but that's what some people say. The one thing I do know is that the glaciers up here are melting, and have been for fifteen years. It's funny to think of an iceberg that's older than Adam and Eve."

From a distance, the island looked as flat and green as a pool table. But the closer we got the more we could see that this was an illusion. The green felt was blemished with countless ripples and cracks.

"That's caused by the permafrost," the Canadian pilot said. "The only way that we can get around is to buy some ATVs."

The Australians looked at each other, then at the pilot. He nodded. They nodded too. Donald Montague said, "We can do that. That's no problem. What's an ATV?"

The pilot explained that these were tricycles with oversized mud-boggler wheels that the Eskimos used for transportation when they weren't using dog sleds or snow machines. "We also need tents, sleeping bags, sunglasses, and lots of food. You go snowblind if you don't wear sunglasses. The pack ice gets so bright that it's almost as bad as looking at the sun. You think you're going to be okay, and then there you are. You see red for a while and then you're blind as a bat. It goes away if you're lucky, but you don't need luck if you've got sunglasses."

I scanned the pilot for vital signs, a stifled smile, or a playful wink—any indication that he might be kidding. He was not. I didn't have any sunglasses and had no real prospects of getting a pair.

Donald said, "I just had an idea."

The Gripper forced a cough to cover up another sort of sound he didn't want Donald to hear. Donald heard it anyway and didn't like it much. They were having one of those silent conversations that old friends have sometimes. Donald said, "Here's what we're going to do. We get to Goatliving—"

"It's Gjoa Havn, eh?" the pilot said.

". . . We get there, stretch our legs, and see the what's what. I'm going to check the prices of sunglasses and food and things like that to see how they go against the price of things back at Fort Franklin, especially those ATVs. They sound like they might take a big bite of my funds. Here's what I figure. Depending on what the prices are, it might be better to drop the Gripper off to keep an eye on the situation so we can fly back to Fort Franklin and buy those ATVs. I work too hard for my money to throw it all away. I bet these Eskimos really put it to you when you got the money and they got the goods."

The Gripper heaved a heavy sigh, and this time there was no mistaking his meaning. The Canadian pilot said, "That's okay with me. I'd rather be flying any day than watching a bunch of scientists Vibroseise the permafrost. Just don't try to save any money when it's time to be paying me, eh, or you and the Gripper'll be floating back to Oz on the Iceberg Express."

Donald nodded, which made it official. The Gripper sighed again. I looked out the plane window. I tried to avert my eyes from the blinding effects of the pack ice, but sometimes I couldn't help myself. I saw two icebergs collide in a great splash of white foam and crushed ice, like a Marguerita Grande that makes you drunk on light.

Gjoa Havn is located in the southeast corner of King William Island, where the channel separating the place from Canada widens into open sea. From 3,500 feet, the island looks like a green quilt made of odd-shaped remnants stitched together by someone who really didn't give a damn. The color comes from the tundra plants that cover the place during the brief interlude of summer. The patchwork pattern is a result of the heaving and shifting that happens when the ground freezes and thaws. Or at least that's what the Canadian said.

"The dark lines that you see cutting through the green are really little gullies and ditches, eh? What happens is the middle heaves up when it freezes and then the sides cave in when it thaws. Pingos and polygons. The whole island looks like that, except for where the village is."

I said, "What's a pingo?"

"It's sort of like a permafrost pimple, a frost heave that's out of control."

Donald said, "Thanks for the lesson, mate, but I quit school more than twenty years ago and I'm too old to go back. Now how about we land this plane?"

We landed on a dirt road that ran parallel to a gravel beach. The icebergs that clogged the waters offshore looked a lot bigger and a lot brighter at sea level. We watched and listened for a minute or two. The blue mountains glided in deadly quiet until two of them collided, and then it sounded as if the earth itself were cracking open.

The village was about three miles up the beach.

Frankie and Donald led the way, followed by the Gripper and me. The pilot stayed back to watch the plane.

"Can't you walk any faster than that?" the Gripper said to me.

"Not on ground like this, but say, you don't have to wait for me."

But, of course, he did have to wait for me because Donald had told him to. He sucked some air through his rotting teeth and picked up a piece of litter from the beach—the plastic top from a tub of margarine. He tossed it Frisbee-style into the ice-clogged sea and watched as the tide pushed it back ashore. By then I was about two hundred yards farther up the beach. He picked up his Frisbee again and trotted after me. He said, "So tell me, sport. What's your angle? I hope Frankie didn't promise you a share of his goods. If he did you'll never see a penny."

"I don't have an angle."

The Gripper didn't quite know how to take this. So he threw his Frisbee back into the sea. I walked ahead while he waited for the sea to return it to him. When it did he picked it up and trotted after me. "What do you mean you don't have an angle? Everybody's got an angle."

"I don't have an angle, I'm telling you. Frankie was going to be on my radio show until you guys canceled us."

The Gripper pondered his margarine Frisbee. Should he throw it into the sea or leave it on the beach? He used it to tap the side of his head. "But the show's the angle I'm talking about. His sister was on it too. I bet that those two're in cahoots and you're their middleman. You're dead if it's true. Donald'll see to that, although I might have to do the dirty work."

"What sister are you talking about? You mean that Dr. Godwin is Frankie's sister?"

I looked around for my own Frisbee but had to settle for a flat skipping stone. I gave it a sidearm throw I'd learned from Bob Locker, a White Sox pitcher who won a few games when I was a boy. The rock skipped a few times before crashing into a chunk of ice.

The Gripper looked at the margarine container top, then looked back at me. "They're brother and sister, all right. There must be a lot that you don't know and that makes you about the biggest chump that I think I've ever seen. What're you doing on Frankie's team if you're not part of the caper?"

My question exactly. Several others crossed my mind, but only Frankie and his sister could answer them. I asked the Gripper a question I was pretty sure he could answer. "So who's Ned Kelly?"

He flung his plastic Frisbee one more time. It bounced off a wave and settled into a pool of foam. The Gripper didn't bother to wait for it this time. We could see Gjoa Havn up ahead, a few dozen mobile homes arranged around a Quonset hut in no particular order. The hut displayed a big sign that informed us we were approaching the Hudson Bay Company Store.

"Ned's not a who. He's a what. He used to be a who back in the bad old days when Oz was a penal colony. But now he's just a what. The gang kept his name out of respect for what he did."

"What was that? What did he do?"

The Gripper said, "Ned Kelly was a bushranger back in the old days. He stole thousands of sheep from the big farmers and then sold them all back to the little farmers for a very tidy profit. He was a typical

Irishman, so he fancied himself a writer and whenever he stole somebody's sheep he always called it politics. The problem is if you steal sheep you stink like sheep so the blues could smell him a mile away. He tried to start a convict rebellion, but the blues cornered him over by Glenrowan. It took a hundred Brits to kill him, though. He died from multiple gunshot wounds in this black iron armor suit that he'd made from the belly of an old wood stove.

"Ned's a hero to lots of people, especially the boys in this gang I'm in. When we talk about Ned Kelly's share, we're really talking about our mates. A man's got to take care of his mates, especially in our line of work where your mate can squeal and send you to the penny. That's the problem with Frankie. He ain't got no mates. Except for his sister, maybe, if it's true they're in cahoots."

The scientists and their TV companions had pitched camp behind the Hudson Bay Company Store. In the middle of the camp was the Vibroseise Device, wired for sound and ready to go. Around it were arranged boxes and crates, people and tents, and at least a dozen ATVs parked in a neat little row on oversize tires with zigzag treads.

The store was run by a man named Bob, who was part white, part Eskimo, and of an uncertain age. His skin was wrinkled but it hadn't turned soft and his hair was more black than white. "I hope you people plan to buy something. I got two lookers in here already."

"I'm looking for some cheap sunglasses," I said. He pointed to the back of the store.

We strolled through the Quonset hut at a window-shopper's pace. The shelves were packed with almost everything and sprinkled with dozens of little red signs promising dozens of HBC Specials! Things can get very expensive in a place too cold for trees: reindeer sausage—$11.35 a pound, laundry bleach—$8.95 a pint, diesel fuel—$10.15 a gallon, and men's down parkas in hunter's red—$299.99, value-added tax included.

Bob the clerk said, "The TV people and their scientists all got here yesterday and I sold them a whole bunch of stuff. Food and water, you bet, and some gasoline for their ATVs. And some extra blankets and firewood and bullets for their guns. You'll be needing that stuff too. And I'm renting them my best bear dog so they don't get caught unawares and get ripped into bite-size pieces. You guys'll need a bear dog too. You're lucky I've got another one that's real good. You can have her for a real good price, eh?"

The Gripper said, "Must be a pretty tough dog to scare off a polar bear."

"Hell no. You crazy," Bob the clerk replied. "Polar bear is never scared of anything. You never try to kill a polar bear with anything less than an elephant gun. I always use an M-16. Polar bears're big and strong and a small gun just pisses them off. The reason you need a polar bear dog is to bark if a bear's coming close. Otherwise a polar bear'll sneak up on you and rip you to shreds before you even know he's there. We've got lots of bears on King William Island. What we don't have a lot of is good bear dogs. I'll rent you one of mine for a hundred dollars a day. What do you say to that?"

The Gripper said that he didn't have any money for a polar bear dog. The clerk put on a worried look and led me over to the cheap sunglasses. Cheap is a relative term, of course. Clip-on shades were $24.95 a pair. I handed over most of my money and attached them to my glasses. The store looked black when the shades were down so I flipped them into the "up" position. Bob thanked me for the purchase and started to tidy up a shelf full of kitchen utensils.

Donald and Frankie were over by a wall that was covered from floor to ceiling with large packing crates. Donald said to Frankie, "I'm not going to pay a price like that."

"We'd be losing time," Frankie replied.

"We'd be losing time but saving money. I think I can live with a deal like that, since I'm the one with all the greenies. Your sister can't be too far gone. They haven't even set up their Vibroseise Device. What about you, Grip? What've you got to say?"

The Gripper said, "You're a bleeding cheapskate, Donald, but I know that you're not going to change your ways."

We stepped outside the Quonset hut and took a roundabout route back to the beach. I flipped down my brand-new shades, which lent a dark purple hue to the bright blue ice. We crossed a patch of lush tundra that felt like a wet sponge beneath our feet and had to hop over the narrow trenches that divided it into pingos and polygons. Frankie said to Donald, "Maybe we should get one of those polar bear dogs. Sounds like it might be useful in a pinch."

"Hell no," Donald said. "I don't even pay the Gripper that much money a day. I pay that much money for a dog and he'll never stop complaining."

"I'm not complaining," the Gripper said. "Let's take a think about this. I don't want to get eaten by any polar bear."

Donald took a think about it, then announced: "Hell no. I'm not paying that kind of money for a dog.

Fifty bucks, maybe, but not a hundred. This place charges too much for everything. They want two thousand dollars for an elephant gun and lots more for an ATV. Let's go back to Fort Franklin and do our shopping there."

I always thought thieves were a free-spending lot— easy come, easy go. Spend some on women, some on booze, and gamble the rest away. I was wrong about that, at least in the case of Donald Montague. The Gripper was disconsolate. His job was to guard Frankie and me without the services of a polar bear dog.

"Tell you what you do, sport," Donald Montague said, nodding at a mangy dog tied up in front of the Hudson Bay Company Store. "You listen to that dog over there, and if he barks you'll know there's a polar bear coming your way."

Donald forced a laugh, hoping it would set the Gripper at ease. It didn't. "We'll be back in less than a day," Donald said. "So you just sit down with your chums and suck down a case of foaming frosties. We'll be back before you're sober."

The Gripper drank his foaming frosties with grim determination. There was no jolly talk of draining the dragon or shaking hands with the unemployed. He was pouring himself a serious drunk. After a while he said to Frankie, "I'm going to take me a nap. You keep an eye on the Radio Star. Maybe we'll all get lucky and he'll get eaten by a polar bear."

Frankie and I walked around. I flipped my shades up and down depending on what I was looking at: up for looking at tundra and the village—down for looking at the iceberg regatta. There wasn't much to see. King William Island is so flat that you can stand on the west beach and see the ice pack off the east beach, which Frankie guessed was about seventy-five miles away. Frankie said, "It's as flat as a table that was just wiped clean. How do these Eskimos live up here?"

I sure didn't know, so I flipped my shades down and shrugged my shoulders to that effect. "You forgot to tell the Speaker that this is all just a family feud."

"He forgot to ask me. Besides, it isn't really. I'd hate Bev even if she wasn't my sister. That woman is poison."

"Maybe so," I said. "But I'm going over to her camp anyway. Are you going to stop me?"

He smiled and shook his head no in a way that made me wish he'd frowned and nodded yes.

Frankie knew his sister well. When I arrived at the camp, she was deep in conversation with some of the people from "Science Today." Other scientists scurried around, rearranging things and loading supplies onto the fleet of ATVs. They were getting ready to leave on the next leg of their expedition, but I would not be joining them. As soon as Dr. Godwin laid eyes on me, she excused herself from her conversation with the TV people and stomped over to me, followed by three big guys with advanced degrees. The biggest, hairiest guy said, "Dr. Godwin here thinks that you're some kind of a snoop. Well, a snoop's as bad as a thief when you're talking about scientific research. So you just bugger off, all right?"

"Just let me talk to Dr. Bud, okay? He's a friend of mine."

Dr. Godwin adjusted her own sunglasses. I could see myself in the reflection of their mirrored lenses. My sunglasses made me look like a nerd. She said, "I'm sorry, Mr. Riordan, but you're not talking to anybody. This camp is off-limits to crooks, reporters, and other creeps. You go tell Frankie that he better stay out of my way or Billy here's going to smack his scrawny arse."

Frankie was over at the Hudson Bay Company Store, chatting about this and that with the wife of Bob the clerk, whose name was Margaret. I had about twelve dollars left in my pocket and resolved to spend it then and there before we went someplace that didn't have any stores. Margaret sold me a canned tuna sandwich and all the coffee I could drink.

"Are you guys scientists too?" she asked. "Or maybe even TV people? I heard somebody say that they're going to make a TV show."

Frankie said, "Yea, that's right. We're TV people, except for Pres here. He's an Alaska radio star. We're making what's called a documentary."

Margaret smiled. "So put me on TV. If you're looking for a lot of frozen stiffs, then I've got a story for you. It's an old family story that Gramma Nelchina used to tell."

Frankie looked nervous so I helped him out. "Tell us the story first so we can think about it. That's the way TV works because videotape is so expensive. These TV guys never ask a question unless they know the answer already."

Some people will do a lot just to get on TV. Margaret did a little. She recited her story in the calm monotone that Eskimos use to describe birth, death, and everything in between. Each fact was carefully put in its proper place, as if she'd been telling the story all her life. Her words had the smooth rhythm that can only be acquired through a lifetime of practice, like vibrato on a violin.

"My Old Ones lived here for all eternity, since the Great Ice Monster melted away. Way back when, long before those who live now were born, the People shared this place with the whales and the seals and the walrus and the bears and the birds and the fish and the sun and the stars and the moon. Then one day, the Old Ones saw a remarkable thing: a long line of white men dragging big boats full of unimportant things.

"Most of the white men were dancing with death. They left a trail of bodies all along the coast. Our dogs ate their meat and left their bones to the sea. The Old Ones feared for the health of their dogs because many of the white men had a disease that made them crazy and caused them to spit out their teeth. One of the white men still had strength to fight the night. The white men called him Captain Crozier. The Old Ones called him Aglooka, which means He Who Speaks Wisdom With A Stick.

"The Old Ones asked Aglooka why he was strong and the others were weak and he said he was like the People, and knows how fire kills the life in food. 'Our canned meat was poisoned,' he said. 'And those who ate it are going to die.'

"This was most certainly so. And all of the white men died, except for Captain Crozier, who became of the People and was called Aglooka and lived with us on King William Island. His Eskimo wife was fat and full of life. She blessed him with four healthy children. The children of their children's children still live among us today. Their eyes are gray and their hair is brown and curly like the tundra gets when winter comes."

Frankie was so excited by this story that his hands began to tremble. "Did you tell this story to any of the scientists?"

Bob answered on his wife's behalf. "She tells it to everybody that's got a minute to spare. Come back tomorrow and she'll tell you again."

Frankie's hands were still trembling, but he wasn't so excited anymore. Margaret said, "That lady scientist liked my story and recorded it on tape."

"Dr. Godwin?" Frankie said.

Margaret nodded. "Yea, I think that's her name. She's very tall and skinny. Like most white women only more so. She said she collects Eskimo stories and wants to write a book some day."

Bob came over with his coffeepot and splashed some into my cup. "When did you talk to these scientists?"

Bob thought about it. "Early in the morning yesterday. They flew in on the big green plane that's parked behind the store. They've got this big machine that pounds the ground and makes my body tingle. They came in and bought many things. They must have plenty of supplies. My wife started flapping jaw with the big white woman and then they went on their way, back to the camp they've got out back."

The Gripper was hunched over another foaming frostie when we got back to the camp. He was a quiet, angry drunkard, the kind who squeeze their anger until it explodes. "I wonder if it's true what they said about them eating people pie."

"Who's that?" Frankie said.

I ducked. The Gripper almost exploded. "The Franklin Expedition, you pommy bastard. Your nine times great-great grandfather. Donald said when they started to starve some of them had a piece of people pie. He said some American found a pot full of human bones. They were bloody cannibals and they didn't even try to hide it. I'd bury the bones if it was me. We need to respect the dead."

You could almost hear the silence that ensued. Frankie's eyes darted around the campfire. First to the Gripper, then to me, and back and forth again. I think my eyes must have done the same. The Gripper's eyes didn't move at all. They were fastened on the can of a foaming frostie he'd crumpled with one hand. "What happens to us if they crash the plane and don't come back? We'd be stuck here with no money, no transportation, and nothing but a bag of potato chips to eat."

"The Eskimos'd feed us."

"What if they don't?"

We all three slept together in a two-man tent that Donald had reluctantly purchased. Frankie put his feet in my face, and the Gripper's elbow played my ribs like a hot jazz xylophone. I didn't get a lot of sleep that night.

CHAPTER 16

Even with sunglasses on, high noon at the top of the world is like looking at a light bulb from the inside out. The pack ice glows like a filament and there are no shadows in which to hide. We could hear the ATVs, but we could see where they were headed.

Frankie said, "It sounds like a motorcar race. I'd say ten vehicles at the very least."

"If I had to say I'd say fifteen. It's like they're a very posh biker gang."

Frankie became very excited. "This is it, Grip. The chase is on. It seems like she's headed north up the coast so I bet she's headed someplace else. That's one thing to know about my sister. She's always got an angle she's working on."

"Just like you, right?" the Gripper said.

Frankie laughed it off. "She's the poise in poison, boys. Hey, Pres. I made a rhyme. I should do the poem on Sir John's statue. I couldn't do worse than the poem they've got."

Now that the Gripper was sober again, everything was a bother; especially me. He said, "I got an angle of my own now, Frankie. I say we uses this stiff for a polar bear dog. Then he can earn his keep."

They discussed the question at length, carefully weighing the pros and cons. It would solve the problem of my position in the group. I was a nowhere man in no place. They didn't want to let me go, but they didn't want to feed me either. Donald was too cheap for that and the Gripper was too hungry. Frankie lobbied effectively against the suggestion that I be killed.

"That's why we use him as a polar bear dog. He'd be dead but we wouldn't kill him. Just like you done to Delbert and Neil when you led them and Donnie out on the mud. Don't tell Donnie I said so, but that was a bonzer move. It'll get you in the Crawler Hall of Fame as far as I'm concerned. How did you ever figure that out?"

Frankie denied the allegation, but accepted the compliment. He promised not to tell Donnie.

The plane was full of expensive supplies: food, blankets, tents, guns, ammunition, two all-terrain vehicles, and an extra pair of sunglasses for all around, myself excepted, of course.

The Gripper counted the people, and he counted the ATVs. "What're you doing, Donnie?"

The tall man had just stepped out of the plane. He stretched his limbs and took a few practice swings at the air. His shoulders didn't seem to hurt anymore.

"Donnie, I'm talking to you. What are you doing to me?"

"Come on, Grip. I don't want to fight." He took a

132

swing at his friend, missing his nose by a fraction of an inch.

The Gripper gave him a jailhouse stare. "You don't want to fight me, mate, because you know I'll bust your arse."

Donald switched to jumping jacks. "Look, Grip. We don't all need a vehicle. Not at the prices they charge. I've got it all worked out. Let me tell you the plan and then you'll understand."

The plan was to track the scientists by air and follow them on the ground. Donald retrieved some boxes from the plane. In them were two sets of two-way radios.

"I laid out a big load of greenies for these so's we could keep in touch. It was still cheaper than an ATV. The problem with a two-way radio is that it only goes two ways. So here's the way it works. The Canuck goes upstairs and scouts out the situation. When he sees something we need to know about, he calls you on the one two-way radio. Then you call us with the news on the other two-way so that everybody knows what's going on. Am I making any sense to you?"

The tundra made a wet, squishy sound as the Gripper paced back and forth. He nodded at me and said, "What about the Radio Star?"

Donald thought about it for a second, then whispered something to the Canadian pilot. The pilot whispered something back and Donald said at last, "That's your job—to keep an eye on him. These radio people are always flapping jaw. We don't want him walking around talking about the goods."

Donald and Frankie left right away, heading north up the eastern coast. The Gripper and I camped on the beach near where the pilot had parked the plane. A few hours later we watched him climb into the sky and then settled down for another long wait. "You better not cause any trouble," he said. "Things'll go bad if you do."

Things were already as bad as I cared them to be. Donald had left behind a miserly supply of essentials: a gun, a tent, some Blasto, a bag of groceries, and the two-way radios. The Gripper guarded these things with more care than he guarded me. He was particularly concerned about the groceries. When I asked him for a bite to eat he announced that I was going on a diet. "There's only food for one here, sport. You're not the one, I'm afraid."

I watched an armada of icebergs float by. Their slow progress made me feel dizzy, as if the world were spinning around me. The two-way radio crackled to life:

    Pilot: This is Fly-boy to Groundhog. What's the story? Over.

    Gripper: There is no story. Over.

    Pilot: Well, I've spotted some eggheads about twenty miles up the coast. They've set up camp between two pingos and they're digging some holes in the ground with some kind of machine that produces a lot of steam. They're probably using a thermal bore. It could be that maybe they found something. Over.

    Gripper: I'll tell Donald as soon as he calls. He's heading in that direction. Over.

The Canadian pilot made a quick calculation of time, distance, and speed. He figured that in three hours, maybe four, Donald and Frankie would reach the place where the scientists had pitched their camp.

The Gripper said that was fine with him, then said, "Over and out."

"I've had about enough of that rod walloper," the Gripper said to me. I was curious to know which rod walloper was testing his patience but decided not to ask. Instead I listened to my stomach growl as he made himself a dinner of instant potatoes and reindeer sausage cooked over a Blasto fire. The jellylike fuel smelled like an oil spill, but the Gripper didn't seem to mind. He wolfed down seven sausages and a large pile of potatoes and washed it all down with a few foaming frosties.

The longer we waited the quieter he became. It was a deadly quiet, like the kind the icebergs made. The two-way radio crackled back to life:

Donald: This is Big Wheel calling Groundhog. Do you read me? Over.

Gripper: I'm right here where you left me, Wheel. Tell me what's going on. Over.

Donald: We just caught up with the eggheads about fifteen minutes ago. They've got a camp on the beach about twenty miles north of where you are now. They're sleeping now but it looks like they dug a bunch of holes in the ground. Have you heard from Fly-boy? Over.

The Gripper gave Donald a detailed report of what the pilot had said. Donald wanted to know what a thermal bore was, but the Gripper didn't have the slightest idea. They made plans to talk the next day, then said, "Over and out."

"I've had about enough of that rod walloper," the Gripper said again.

This time I knew who he meant. "Have another

foaming frostie," I suggested. "It'll do you a world of good."

He had another and another and another, as the vanishing light of the arctic night turned the green land, the blue sky, and the white sea into different shades of gray. I flipped up my shades, curled up near the Blasto fire, and pretended to sleep on the ground. The Gripper slurped another beer and talked to himself about many important things—his past, his future, his position in the Ned Kelly Gang. After about an hour of this, he dropped his last beer can, slumped over, and started to snore. I looked at my watch when I was sure that he was sound asleep. It was 1:35 A.M. back on the Bodenburg Butte. I wondered what day it was. Sunday, I think. But who knows in a place like this?

Slowly, and without making a noise, I started to crawl away from the beach in the general direction of the Hudson Bay Company Store. At first the ground was cold and hard. Odd pieces of gravel scraped and poked me as I dragged myself along. Then the ground was wet and hard, as I moved onto the carpet of tundra plants that made up the part of the island that wasn't beach.

Just when I was becoming confident in my escape, my elbow crushed a little something that made a pathetic squeak. I took a close look all around me and saw that the tundra was infested with thousands of little rodents each of which was equipped with a set of beady little eyes. They squirmed and squealed and munched on tundra plants as I blundered into their boggy habitat. It was like crawling through a rats' nest, but I did not dare stand up and run for it for fear that the Gripper would see me.

My escape was also complicated by the network of

cracks in the surface that divided the tundra into pingos and polygons. Most of the cracks were a few feet thick and a few feet deep, but some were much bigger than that. Climbing in and out of these cracks was a dirty and difficult chore, all done with my head down low and moving to the music of rodents at feast. One time the crack was deeper than I was tall, and the sides were so muddy and slick that I was unable to pull myself out. So I followed the crack around the pingo that it encircled, until it intersected with another crack that wasn't so deep.

I checked my watch again when I was back on level ground. It was 2:15 A.M. back on the Bodenburg Butte. I could see lights in the night up ahead, but I couldn't tell how far away they were. I jumped to my feet and started to run, or at least I started the hop-shuffle-skip that is my way of moving fast. Tundra plants and rodents were crushed beneath my shuffling feet. I vaulted over the cracks and splashed through the boggy puddles that gathered in the low spots between the polygons and pingos. But the lights didn't seem any closer when the howling of a bear dog stopped me in my tracks.

Haoooooooweeeeeee-yap-yap-yap.

Another dog howled, and another one howled back. In a moment the night was filled with the noise of a hundred frightened dogs. I hoped they were howling at me, instead of at a polar bear. Somebody said, "Hey you! What're you doing out there?"

I looked in the direction of the voice. Another light had pierced the gray. It was much brighter and closer than the lights I was running toward.

I said, "I'm sorry. I guess I got lost."

"That's exactly right, you're lost. You're standing on my property. Walk over to the light."

The light was coming from the window of a tiny shack. The shack was made of tin and covered with animal skins. When I got close enough to knock on the door, the man with the voice stuck a gun in my back. "You must be one of those science people that came here the other day."

"No, I'm not. I'm a . . . I'm a . . . You know, what I really am is hungry. Do you have any food to eat?"

The voice and the gun belonged to a man named Albert MacDonoghue. He was a purchasing agent for the Amalgamated Furriers of the Northwest Territories. He filled me up with coffee and beans and told me all about it.

"I get arctic foxes and polar bears and then sell them to the shops in Montreal. You wouldn't think to look at it, but Gjoa Havn is the center of something. I get furs from all around. There's trappers over on the mainland that come to me to sell their goods, and the Eskimos got the islands covered. There's lots of seals and polar bears, if you haven't figured that out yet. I can sell you a polar bear rug and give you a real good price. Take it from me, lad. Women want to get naked whenever they see a polar bear rug."

"I don't think so," I replied. "I'm a little short of cash right now."

MacDonoghue took my plate and dropped it into the bucket that he used as a kitchen sink. "So if you're not one of them scientists, then what're you doing here? Nobody comes here if they don't have a reason."

I told the man my troubles, starting with Danger Dan, continuing with the Australian thieves, and finishing with the rodents. He said, "Those would be a kind of lemming, son. It's a teeny-tiny arctic mouse that lives off the tundra plants. Every now and then they jump into the sea. I can't say that I blame them. It's a pretty hard life up here, but they do all right. There's millions of lemmings on King Will's Island. The pelts aren't worth a damn, though. There's not a lot of call for mouse-skin coats. I don't understand these scientists."

"How's that?" I said.

"We get a group of scientists that comes up here every now and then. This year it's these Australians. Two years ago it was these Canadians. They all come looking for the very same thing, anything left behind by the Franklin Expedition, especially books and photographs. They say they're trying to find out what happened to Sir John, but that's the part that don't make sense because they already know what happened. He got stuck in the ice and had a heart attack, then his men got the scurvy and starved. So if they already know what happened, then they must be looking for something else. I think they're looking for a secret treasure. That would explain your Australian thieves. I don't think I ever met a thief yet who gave a damn about learning. What do you think about that?"

I checked my watch. It was 4:13 A.M. back on the Bodenburg Butte. "I think I'd better get going before the Gripper wakes up."

The night had left some clouds behind and the sea was covered with fog. The lemmings were still munching away, but the dogs had settled down. As I came up to the scientists' camp, the Herc C-130 was quiet and still, as were the tents that it had delivered to this godforsaken place. Most of the ATVs were gone, but the Vibroseise Device still presided over a large pile of boxes and packing crates. The camp was guarded by a small Australian with a large gun that he pointed at my head.

"Who goes there?" the Australian said.

"Prester John Riordan," I replied.

"And who the hell is that?"

"I'm a friend of Dr. Bud, the guy who's flying that plane. I've got to see him right away."

"Come back later. Bud's still asleep," the small Australian said. He emphasized his point by waving the gun at me. I headed for the Hudson Bay Company Store. The sign said it was closed.

I hadn't counted on this. I'd planned to throw myself on the mercy of Bob the clerk or Margaret, his wife. I'd beg them to call the Mounties or at least let me borrow their telephone. Then something good would happen, and everything would be okay. It wasn't much of a plan, but I didn't have much of a choice.

The sign on the store said it opened at eight o'clock, but that didn't help me much. It was almost 5 A.M. on the Bodenburg Butte, but what time was it here? Time doesn't mean much in a place like this, where the sun shines at midnight, the sky goes on forever, and frozen bodies are kept on ice for more than a hundred years.

I sat on the steps of the company store and started to wait for Bob. My mind began to wander and drift until it impaled itself on Lindy Sue Reef.

I'd been living a happy life before Lindy Sue came along. Rachel and I would walk along the beach and talk about the future. Happy people talk about the future. Sad ones talk about the past. Rachel and I would talk about the time when we would own a small newspaper and charge exorbitant rates to well-heeled advertisers. Rachel wanted to have a baby and I wanted to be a baby, but we always knew we'd work it out until Lindy Sue came along. I started to have impure thoughts of such number and magnitude that I felt like I was thirteen years old again. Thoughts are thoughts and deeds are deeds. We did it on the beach. Rachel found out when I confessed and kicked me out of the house. I found out later that she was pregnant with the baby she wanted to have. I haven't seen her since.

Howeeeeeeeeee! Yoweeeeeeeeee! Yap! Yap! Yap!

Suddenly the big sky that went on forever became filled with the noise of a hundred frightened dogs. Maybe it was a polar bear and maybe it was the Gripper waking from his drunken sleep. I was in trouble in either case. If it was a bear, he'd rip me to shreds and eat me from the inside out. If it was the Gripper, he'd have a hangover and be in an ugly mood. I looked around for a place to hide, but the island was as flat as it ever was. The shacks offered no hiding place, as they were all guarded by frightened dogs.

I jumped to my feet and ran around back to the scientists' camp. The little man with the big gun was still guarding the place, walking back and forth with his weapon at the ready. "You here again," he said. "What do you want this time?"

"I've still got to talk to Dr. Bud. It's about the Franklin Expedition."

"Righto! Hang on a jiff, will you, sport?"

He was looking at something off in the distance, beyond the flat expanse of pingos and polygons. "It looks like your chum's coming too this time."

I followed his gaze to a distant figure climbing out of a crack in the ground. The Gripper was on his way. Before I could tell the guard that he was my captor and not my friend, the scientist pointed his gun in the air and shot off a single round. The Gripper stopped moving for a moment, to think about what this meant. Then he continued to come our way—at a faster pace, I think.

The shot had wakened the rest of the camp. Scientists started to crawl out of their tents, still wearing their nightclothes and bearing arms of various sorts: a slender woman with a robe and pistol and a hairy man with bikini briefs and a hunting knife, a fat man in a nightshirt with a shotgun, and a black man in pajamas with a boomerang.

Then there was Dr. Bud. He was wearing boxer shorts and his colonel's hat from the Alaska National Guard. Instead of a weapon he had in his hands a two-way radio. This one looked much fancier than the two-ways used by the thieves. It had a longer antenna and lights that blinked when he spoke:

Dr. Bud: This is base camp to Digger. I think we've got it under control. It looks like an old friend of yours: Prester John Riordan. You remember him. He's the guy from Alaska who put you on his radio show. Over.

Dr. Godwin: I remember him all right. I kicked him out of the camp right before we left. He must be working with my twithead brother, so he can't be up to any good. Find out what he wants and then get rid of him. Over and out.

Half of the group waited for the Gripper to arrive while the other half took me into a field tent that was big enough to hold a circus, but colored a somber gray. The interior looked a lot like a children's science fair, with portable tables on which were displayed the results of many projects in which logic and whimsy were attempting to make common cause: tundra wilting under artificial light, a collection of local rocks, the fossilized skull of something with teeth. They sat me down in a folding chair next to a table with a specimen jar. A dead lemming was pickled in clear white liquid. It looked like it wanted to squirm and squeal.

"What're you doing here, Pres?" Dr. Bud said to me.

His colleagues crowded around as I told him all about it. The hairy man in the bikini briefs didn't believe a word I said. His name was Kinsley Crawford. He had earned his letters in something called photogrammetrics. "He's a genuine dinki-di liar, I'd say. We should kick him out of camp, just like Beverly told us to do."

"You do everything Beverly says," the black man with the boomerang said. "She leads you around by your tummy banana."

The other scientists laughed, especially Kinsley Crawford.

"I don't think he's lying," Dr. Bud said. "I've known Pres for a pretty long time and he never seemed like a thief to me. I think he's telling the truth."

Before I had a chance to agree, one of the other scientists stepped inside the tent. He was unarmed and fully dressed, a mammalian biologist named Thomas Crocker. He'd written many papers about the social habits of the dingo, a wild Australian dog. He said, "The other thief stopped moving. He's sitting on top of a pingo about two hundred yards away. He must be waiting for this one, I guess."

143

Kinsley Crawford said, "See what I mean. And even if he's not working with them, he's not doing us any good."

"That's not true," I said. "I think I can help you a lot."

The ensuing hubbub gave me a chance to think of something to say. "I figure as long as I'm here, I'll write a story for the *New York Times.*"

Kinsley said to Dr. Bud, "I've heard about that sheet. Yanks with lots of money read it."

This time Dr. Bud was the one who didn't believe me, but he didn't let his friends know that. "That's right, Kinsley," he replied. "And government people read it too. Any U.S. research scientist who's trying to get a grant would love to be in the *New York Times.* A story by Pres could do wonders for your work in photogrammetrics. He could tell people that there is such a thing."

"That might be all right," Kinsley Crawford said.

Their mood changed as quickly as that. Now they all wanted to be my friend, especially the fat man in the nightshirt. "Jimbo Cooper's my name. Allow me to show you my tundra plants. Some of them are quite remarkable."

"Shouldn't you put on some clothes first."

Everybody finally noticed that no one but me was fully clothed. They cleared out of the lab and scurried back to their tents, leaving me with Dr. Bud. My friend adjusted his colonel's hat and stood at ease in his boxer shorts.

"The *New York Times?*" he said. "You're lucky they're all from Australia or they'd laugh you right off this island."

"I just said I was writing a story. I didn't say they'd

print it. Somebody'll print it, though. Aussie eggheads dig up last remains of English cannibals. How's that for a headline? Sounds like the latest edition of the *National Enquirer.*"

Bud smiled. "Or maybe a sign on Danger Dan's truck."

CHAPTER 17

The Gripper was sitting on an enormous pingo. A geologist named Johnny Grimes told me all about pingos.

"I've never seen anything like it myself. Oz never gets cold enough for the ground to freeze like that. What happens is the topsoil freezes in the fall and melts again in the spring. Sometimes the ground gets so wet that it'll expand when it freezes again, like water in an ice cube tray. Think of an ice cube tray filled with mud that's mostly water. Set your freezer at forty below and you'll have yourself a tray full of pingos. I wonder how come he's just sitting out there."

"He's waiting for me, I guess."

"We'll let him wait," the botanist said. "You tell me about the *New York Times* and I'll show you my tundra plants. I'm working on a theory that plants from other continents can be adapted to conditions in the Outback of Australia. Oz is mostly desert, you

146

know. Some greenery would sure brighten things up. All we've got is grass and scrub and this weed we call the saltbush."

Of course, he had to tell me all about saltbush. It was a lot more than I wanted to know. The geologist gave me a look that implied that the botanist was a bit of a crank. But he seemed determined to show me his tundra plants, so I agreed to look.

His specimens were clearly marked and arranged in alphabetical order: Drummond's dryas, lupine, woolly lousewort. They'd been sprayed with some sort of preservative that killed the plants but preserved their color. The botanist picked up the woolly lousewort. It looked like a lollypop turned to mold.

"Do you know what my dream is, Mr. Riordan? And you can put this in your *New York Times*. I'd like to figure out a way to make the Outback green. Your desert is full of flora. Ours is full of saltbush. I wrote a paper in *Botany Review* about your Yankee cactus. I want my next paper to be about tundra plants. Cactus and tundra have one thing in common. They both live in places where nothing else grows. Half of Oz is a place like that. Do you see what I'm getting at?"

Except for their special obsessions, Australian scientists have many things in common with Australian thieves. They like to eat their food and drink their beer and announce when it's time to relieve themselves. Slash the potatoes. Drain the dragon. Shake hands with the unemployed.

They'd used a thermal bore to dig a pit in the permafrost. With the proper insulation, it made a dandy freezer which they had filled with meat, homemade soup, ice cream, and other perishables. We had ourselves a party. We drank warm beer with tomato juice and ate reindeer meat and real potatoes cooked on what appeared to be the world's biggest barbecue. The Gripper watched us celebrate from his perch atop the pingo.

"Thanks a lot, pal," I said to Dr. Bud.

"What's wrong with you?" he replied. "You should be happy as a lark now that you're working for the *New York Times*. What're you thanking me for?"

"For setting me up, that's what."

"What are you talking about?"

I was talking about the fact that Frankie Stubbs and Dr. Godwin turned out to be brother and sister. I figured that Bud must have known all along. He said I figured wrong.

"I'm as surprised as you. I didn't find out myself until just the other day when all of a sudden everybody starts walking around with guns. I asked 'How come?' and they said they were worried about thieves. I said that I didn't see any thieves so they told me about Frankie Stubbs. I guess he and his sister had a falling-out. I never did get the whole story."

I told him the part of the story I thought I knew. He refused to believe that Frankie Stubbs was descended from the great Sir John. "But his sister, now that's another story. I'd believe a lot about her. That woman is more than ten men can handle. She's twice as smart as everybody else and half the camp is in love with her. The funny thing is they all think that she's in love with them."

"Come on, Bud."

"No, it's true. You'll find out yourself tomorrow. We're heading up the coast to deliver the Vibroseise Device. They dug a few test holes aways up north and Dr. Godwin thinks that maybe they might have found an artifact."

CHAPTER 18

The Hercules C-130 is a plane of truly heroic proportions. It was developed during the Second World War and saw proud service as the packhorse of the American military machine. It could deliver large numbers of men with a heavy load of baggage to distant places in very little time. It was equipped with oversize tires that allowed it to land on something besides concrete, like the gravel beaches of King William Island.

Dr. Bud was proud of his Herc. He showed me the cockpit and read me the official army line. "The Hercules C-130 can deliver two Sherman tanks and three platoons of fighting men into a hostile situation six hundred miles away. It has a top speed of four-fifty per when fully loaded and five-seventy-five per when empty. It is equipped with an automated piloting system, an official Alaska Army National Guard tractor-trailer unit and a Parachute Survive Pak for every man and boy among us. I'd say we're ready for just about anything, Pres."

"What's the tractor-trailer for?"

He studied his gauges for a moment, as if the answer were a function of altitude and fuel supply. "The purpose of the REMTRAC-350 Remote Tractor unit is the transportation of military materiel over irregular terrain. That's a National Guard way of saying we'll use it to haul the Vibroseise Device around once we hit the beach. That'll happen pretty soon. This plane really eats up space."

He was about ready to take off, so I took my place in the belly of the plane. The Vibroseise Device was strapped to the front of the cargo hold and the tractor-trailer was strapped to the back. There were no seats to speak of, just more green straps tied in a loop and suspended from the ceiling. We clung to these like rush-hour commuters crowded into a train. Hanging from straps on either side of me were two Australian scientists—Allan Phillips, the mammalian biologist, and Kinsley Crawford, the photogrammarian. They talked about photographs, carnivores, and photographs of carnivores. I took notes for the story I'd promised to write.

"Let me tell you about what I do," the photogrammarian said. "You can put my story in the *New York Times.*"

Kinsley Crawford could tell when and where a picture was taken by measuring the angle of various shadows and applying a few mathematical equations. He'd written a paper called "Photographic Fraud: A Forensic Review." He was sometimes used as an expert witness by Australian barristers in litigation involving divorce and industrial espionage. He was madly in love with Dr. Godwin, and denied it at every opportunity.

"Sun pictures," he said. "That's what I'll be looking

for. A find like that would make my career because Sir John was the first explorer to take a camera along. I bet that would throw dear Bev for a loop, not that I care, mind you. But it's very exciting, you see. Photography was just getting started back in Sir John's day, and the Frenchies were on the cutting edge. The newspaper accounts of his leaving London say that Lady Jane gave him a daguerreotype machine, which is what the Frenchies used to call a camera. It made pictures on a copperplate. White highlights and pitch-black shadows—very contrasty stuff. But the best thing about daguerreotypes is the images almost never fade. Not like your modern photographs."

I said, "What would a picture like that be worth?"

He added some numbers in his head—big numbers, I suspect, but it took him a little too long. Before he could answer my question, the mammalian biologist launched into a long lecture about polar bears and the Tasmanian devil. "They are both highly specialized carnivores," he eventually concluded. I looked out one of the Herc's windows, at the pingos and polygons passing by below.

Even at 4,500 feet, it was easy enough to follow the trail that the ATVs had made along the eastern shore. The tundra plants had been flattened by the oversize tires. The trail was tinted gray by the smoke of the exhaust.

We followed the coast for a while. Every now and then we would see some hole that the scientists had dug and abandoned. The soft mounds that were created when they filled the holes back in were one of the few distinctive features of the place. King William Island is as deprived of geography as it is of trees. The tundra didn't change much from the soft green carpet we'd seen around Gjoa Havn, and the network of cracks persisted. Other natural features were notable by their absence. There were no hills or valleys because the island had been scraped flat by glaciers of the Great Ice Age.

The icebergs off the south coast were packed so tightly together that an acrobat could have skipped across the channel to mainland Canada, leaping from one ice mountain to another. At the place called Starvation Cove, the icebergs congested into an enormous ice jam and the pack ice made a grinding noise.

Dr. Bud dipped the left wing down so we could get a better look at the iceberg traffic jam. "It's the closest place to the mainland," Kinsley Crawford said. "That's why the ice jams up."

A big chunk of ice cracked free of the pack and started to float away. The scientists gave a beer-hall cheer, as if the icebergs were playing Australian rules football. I wondered what the Gripper was up to. "Why do they call it Starvation Cove?"

The mammalian biologist answered, "They say about a hundred of Franklin's men died of starvation here. They wanted to cross over to the mainland, but they didn't have the strength. Here's where they found evidence that pointed to cannibalism."

The icebergs off the east coast did a slow dance in the open sea. Something came loose in my brain: a thought, a memory, or a notion that would rattle around until it came out. I tapped my head twice with the heal of my hand, as if trying to make a marble fall out of my ear. It turned out to be a steelie that plopped onto the floor of the plane with a sensible, metallic thud. I remembered the story the woman had told us at the Hudson Bay Company Store.

I started my retelling of the Eskimo legend with an

enthusiasm my audience wouldn't sustain. The two scholars had already heard the one about the white man who ate raw meat. Aglooka, a.k.a. Captain Crozier, was an old story with vague beginnings that most of the scientists didn't believe. Dr. Beverly Godwin, the expert in tribal legends, was in the minority, according to the photogrammarian.

"You can ask her about it yourself," he said. "We'll be coming in for a landing soon."

The scientists had smoothed down a landing strip and marked it with red flares. We got a good look at the camp they had pitched as Dr. Bud banked the Herc into a long, sweeping turn for the final approach. They had set up one large tent and lots of little ones, and then circled them with their ATVs. Donald and Frankie huddled off to one side, while a group of scientists were off to another, using a thermal bore to dig a hole in the permafrost.

Dr. Godwin took one look at me and made a sour face. She was wearing knee boots, riding pants, and an Australian bush hat with a feather in the brim. She circled me from right to left, as if I were something caught in a trap she'd set. I told her I was going to write a story for the *New York Times*.

"The *New York Times,* you say. That's very impressive, Mr. Riordan. I'd like to see your credentials, please."

"You'd like to see my what?"

"A business card or a press pass. Some proof that you're not a fraud."

I picked through my wallet for something that looked official. The best I could do was an old pay stub from KREL Kountry Radio, 580 on the AM dial. Two hundred dollars for one week of work, minus taxes for this and that. Dr. Godwin was not impressed. "This man is a charlatan," she said. "Keep him away from me."

I told her I wasn't a charlatan but confessed that the story I intended to write was a speculative venture at best. The botanist seemed disappointed, while the photogrammarian was merely amused.

Dr. Godwin said, "In other words you're a 'writer,' one of the fashionably unemployed. Well, you're not going to write about me, sir. I have an agreement with 'Science Today.' They've got exclusive rights. You came up here with my brother. You can go write your story about him. Sell it to the *Police Gazette*."

They pounded the ground for more than a week and dug dozens of holes in the permafrost. During this period of time, the weather couldn't decide what it wanted to be. High noon was almost warm, almost time to take off our coats and get down to our shirtsleeves. The nights, as short and gray as they were, reminded me of those overcast winter days, when our breath comes out in chilly clouds that seem to contain the makings of snow.

The Vibroseise Device did its work slowly, although I can't say that it was an entirely unpleasant experience. It found something every now and then and the ceaseless pounding of its pile-driver unit kept us all in a somewhat excited state. It invited more than the usual number of impure thoughts, mostly about Dr. Godwin.

She was the darling of the crew from "Science Today." They followed her around like a pack of devoted puppies wired for sight and sound. Her every thought was captured on tape, her every curve preserved in ECU, which is television talk for Extreme CloseUp. The producer was fascinated by the Eskimo stories she told.

"They say the good ship *Terror* floated south for four long years after the crew abandoned it, trapped in the grip of the great ice pack that had doomed the expedition. Then two brothers who were hunting seals spotted this ghost ship off the west coast of Qeqertaq. That's the Eskimo name for King William Island. They pretended the ship was a sleeping seal and tried to sneak up on it. Seeing that it was not occupied, they decided to plunder it of tools and other things of use in their simple lives. They used axes to make a hole so the light would shine in on the cargo area. The *Terror* sank shortly after that."

The TV producer had a long neck and loud voice which allowed him to be seen and heard in a crowd. He stretched out and screeched a command. "I want an ECU right here." Then he said to Dr. Godwin, "Now tell us the legend of Maggie Stubbs."

The ECU looked good but sounded wrong. Dr. Godwin had the understated confidence that women of great beauty possess, but she didn't place any faith in that particular legend. "You don't want to hear about that. That's just the daydream of a naughty little boy who wants to get rich without doing any work."

There are no secrets in a place that flat, with that much nothing to do. I let it be known that even if the *Times* didn't print my story, some publication would. This had a powerful appeal to the scientists who weren't going to be on "Science Today," which is to say most of them.

There were seventeen scholars by my count, not including Dr. Bud who was there as a pilot rather than a seeker of seed-potato truth. In addition to those already named, were a toxicologist, five historians, and anthropologists of various stripes. The botanist had been correct in observing that most of them were infatuated with the lovely Dr. Godwin. This was most annoying to the analytic nutritionist. Her name was Gwynn Mikkelson and she was the only other woman in the group. She was attracted to a certain mammalian biologist who seemed to prefer Dr. Godwin's scorn to her own passionate embraces.

"Bev's the kind of girl that men fear and women hate," Gwynn Mikkelson said. "She can turn a man upside down, slap him around, and then the bloke'll send flowers to apologize. I feel sorry for her brother. He must have got it from get-go. She always gets her way with men no matter how smart they think they are. You could ask her hubby all about that if he wasn't such a basket case."

Her husband was a famous cultural anthropologist, just like Beverly was going to be. He'd been her teacher, in fact, and was some thirty years older than she. At first he was envied by his fellow academics as a salty old dog who'd got himself a tender young hostie in which to dip his wick. Now he was the object of pity and ridicule, the silly old fool who wore his cuckold's horns with grim sobriety.

Gywnn said, "Now there's some people who say she married him to get a respectable name, since the Stubbses are known to be thieves. And then there's other people who say that she's the one that's really a thief. And then there's been some questions raised about a paper she wrote about aboriginal folk tales.

Some people say that her hubby really wrote that paper, but he's too much in love to file a formal complaint. Of course, some people will say just about anything, especially about a woman like Bev."

I spent some time with Dr. Bud, who didn't have much to do, and more time with the pesky botanist, who was determined that I should write about his dream of developing a species of Australian cactus.

"Cacti are very efficient, you know. They have magnificent flowers and can live for years on almost no water at all."

I pretended to write this down, then nodded at a group of scientists who gathered around the Vibroseise Device as it pounded the ground with pile-driver thuds. The lead geologist, who was on loan to the group from Petco, listened through a pair of headphones while an assistant tended to the Vibroseise dial. Several other scientists stood around enjoying the vibrations.

"What have they found so far?" I asked the botanist.

"Well, it's all very interesting, because there seems to be a pattern. They've found the barrel of a British Army rifle and six pieces of silverware—three knives, two forks, and a spoon—that have been positively ascribed to the Franklin Expedition. But that's not the interesting part. The interesting part is the silverware was buried at one-mile intervals. The most exciting theory is that Captain Crozier was laying a trail, dropping bread crumbs so to speak."

"Laying a trail to what?" I said.

"Well, that's the question of the hour. But you don't want to write about that. Let's talk about this project

of mine. The genus *Cactaceae opuntia* seems especially suited to conditions in the Outback."

The botanist was so relentless that I retreated to the
one place where he would never follow: the camp of
the Australian thieves. Frankie and Donald tried to
stay clear of me. I think they were afraid that I'd ask
them for some food. Since I was a part of neither
group, I had to rely on the generosity of those who
hadn't cleaned their plates. A bit of meat here, a bite
of potato there. Dr. Bud was very kind, and so was the
pesky botanist. Frankie and Donald weren't kind at
all. They warmed themselves around a quart of Blasto
and waited for something to happen. The fuel burned
hot for a long, long time, sending clouds of gray into
the blue.

Frankie said, "Something's got to happen soon. It
was real cold last night, and it even got dark for a
while."

Donald said, "Forget about the weather. Let's talk
about the goods."

Ah yes, the goods. And the thousand-yard stare that
the two thieves had whenever they started to dream
about what those goods might be.

"Maybe they're photographs," I suggested.

Donald and Frankie gave me a look that said that I
was crazy, then returned their eyes to things they
could not see in the distance.

"You know what I think it is?" Donald Montague
said.

"What's that?" Frankie replied.

"I think the goods is some real estate Sir Johnny
had way on the outskirts of Sydney."

"That doesn't sound like much. I still think it's a
gold mine."

"Not me," Donald said. "I want it to be real estate. Because whatever was outskirts in Sir John's day is probably 'inskirts' now. Maybe somebody took our land and built a shopping mall on it. We could sue the shopping mall and get rich for the rest of our lives."

"The barristers would get all the money. Gold is better than real estate."

"Just so it's not a sheep ranch," Donald Montague said. "The first time I got arrested they sent me to a sheep ranch run by the blues instead of to the penny. They thought crooks could be cured by work. They were wrong about that, though, because all it did is make me want to never work on a sheep ranch again. The sheep stand around eating grass all day and the people do all the work. First, you've got to dip them. Then you've got to sheer off the wool. That's the hardest part, because wool sheep make a stink that smells like Abbo's pits."

"Who's Abbo?" I asked.

Donald didn't hear the question, as he had already launched into a description of how sheep are dipped in a powerful disinfectant made of creosote, arsenic, and nicotine. This took quite some time and made me swear off wool for life. He was still at it when Frankie noticed that the scientists were breaking camp.

They traveled in single-file behind the tractor-trailer they used to haul the Vibroseise Device. Bud let me ride with the big machine because I didn't have an ATV. The frost heaves and the tundra plants were like a velvet roller coaster. The trail had its ups and downs, but the ride was quiet and smooth when we came up on some lemmings that were feeding on the brownish tundra plants that grew near the eastern beach. Bud tried to avoid the rodents, but found it impossible to do so completely. Those who didn't scamper away made terrified squeaks as they were crushed beneath our wheels.

We covered a mile in thirteen minutes; then it was time to dig again. Dr. Bud turned on the Vibroseise Device and the lead geologist listened through the headphones as the TV producer directed his crew—a film photographer, a sound man, and several other TV men of uncertain purpose. Then they rolled some more tape of Dr. Godwin while Dr. Bud stood off to the side, wishing he had studied something more compelling than virus-free seed potatoes.

About thirty minutes of Vibroseising produced several impure thoughts, but nothing of scientific value. They were about to give it up when the lead geologist said, "I think we've got something."

The lead geologist was a man named Brian, on loan from Petco to operate the device. With him were two lesser geologists who now scurried to their positions by the machine. One monitored a dial and the other listened to a second pair of headphones. "Sounds like something big," the second student said.

"It looks like it's big too," said the student who was watching the dial.

Their leader spoke loudly and slowly, so the TV mikes would pick it up: "We better get the thermal bore."

The thermal bore produced so much steam and so much noise that we couldn't see or hear a thing as it drilled a hole wider than a man into the rock-hard permafrost. When the noise stopped and steam drifted away the lead geologist said, "It's another foot down, whatever it is. We'll have to be careful now."

The hole they'd dug with the thermal bore was

about as deep as a short man's knees. The lead geologist explained his every move to the TV camera. He first declared the place to be an Official Archeological Site, and signed some Canadian document that made it officially so. Then he produced a corrugated tube that blew hot air into the hole he was digging.

"What we're doing is melting the permafrost without damaging whatever is buried down there. What we've got here is rocks and gravel cemented together with ice. What we need to do is melt the ice and loosen the rocks one by one. I'd like to take a pickax to this place but I can't take the chance of damaging the goods. This is going to take some time."

"Science Today" recorded his every word, in case he said something interesting. He never did. By the time he was waist-deep in the hole, even his colleagues were bored. A few of them started cooking dinner while a few more walked down the beach to get a closer look at the ice pack shifting about offshore. The slow passage of the silent mountains was a spectacular sight indeed, especially when they collided.

Dr. Godwin gave up the vigil when the lead geologist took a rest from his digging and launched into a windy discussion of the action of glaciers on King William Island. She excused herself and retired to her tent, followed moments later by the lovesick photogrammarian. As soon as they were out of earshot, the geologists started to laugh, especially the ones who were jealous.

"Kinsley's going to let her bite his tummy banana."

"Prod her with his beef bayonet."

"Crack a fat with Long John Thomas."

The TV producer used his long neck and loud voice to call an end to the festivities. "That's a wrap, guys. Let's pack it up for the night."

The crowd thinned out some more and the "Science Today" people carried their equipment away. The scientists wandered back to their tents, still talking about poor Kinsley Crawford and his romantic escapade.

"Ding her with his donger."

"Exercise the ferret."

"Dip his wick in the old fun bag."

When they were gone, all that remained were Frankie, Donald, the geologists, and me. Donald said he was hungry. Frankie said he wasn't. I didn't say anything. The geologists kept digging.

"You guys go on," Frankie said. "Bring me over a bite to eat and I'll keep an eye on the situation."

Frankie and the geologists became friends of a sort because Frankie stayed with them to the bitter end. Frankie was their only witness when the lead geologist said at the top of his lungs, "Coo-ee! Coo-ee! Looks like we've got something here. I think it's some kind of box."

We all rushed back to the hole we'd dug in the permafrost. "Science Today" was the first to arrive. They were already doing their TV dance by the time Donald and I arrived. Dr. Godwin and her photogrammarian were the last to arrive on the scene. She looked happy while he looked too tired to blow out a candle.

CHAPTER 19

Dr. Godwin supervised the removal of the box from the hole in the permafrost. "Science Today" interviewed the lead geologist about the meaning of it all. He gave full credit to his employer, the Petco Petroleum Company, for allowing the scientists to use the Vibroseise Device.

"I declare this box to be an Official Archeological Artifact under the laws of England and the Dominion of Canada," Dr. Godwin said. She then signed some Canadian papers that made it official.

"Are your people ready?" she said to the TV producer.

The man with the long neck and the loud voice nodded. His people had bathed the area in light and littered it with microphones. "All right. Let's do it then," Dr. Godwin said.

Four younger scientists lowered four sticks into the hole, one on each side of the metal box. The tips of the sticks were adjustable and could be used to get a grip on the bottom of the box. Once the sticks were in their proper places, they secured the protruding ends of these sticks with a lightweight metal cage that stabilized the box while they lifted it into the light of day.

It was a very small box for such a big fuss, but perfectly preserved by the hard freeze of the permafrost. It was made of wooden slats that still seemed supple and held together by metal braces undamaged by rust. The lovesick photogrammarian took a picture of the box while the botanist scraped off a bit of moss that had gathered on the lock. He dipped it into a chemical solution, waited five minutes, and then pronounced it to be a frozen bit of *tripe de roche,* a species of moss common in the northern latitudes.

"Science Today" interviewed an Australian naval historian who described the box as a typical one used by British naval officers in the nineteenth century. "It's the dinki-di genuine article all right, waterproof and very strong. They used it to keep their official papers. It's built to float if the ship goes down, a bit like a message in a bottle. Its purpose is to preserve a record of the voyage. A good skipper keeps a grip on his box until he meets his maker. Then he hands it over to his second in command."

A professor of archeology used one of a dozen skeleton keys to pick the lock on the box. "Science Today" made sure to capture the creaking sound the joints made as he pried open the lid. The box was filled with loose sheets of thick paper. The sheet on top had been scribbled on in a weak and hurried hand. The naval historian read it out loud: "Herein lies the Official Log of Francis R. Crozier, Captain of the HMS *Terror,* which with the HMS *Erebus* became beset by pack ice while on a Royal Voyage of Discovery through the Northwest Passage. We discovered same but many died in so doing. I am the last survivor thanks to the good offices of the Gentle Savages who reside in this vicinity. Good Christian souls who find this box are beseeched by the dead to deliver it into the hands of the British admiralty, so that they might know the fate of Sir John Franklin and his hearty crew of sailors brave."

"Science Today" zoomed in for an Extreme Close-Up as the rest of us crowded around for a closer look at the historic artifact. Some of the pages were yellow but seemed otherwise untouched by time. The permafrost had preserved the ship's log, if not its captain. He'd started writing in a strong and confident hand that weakened and worried as time went on. The log covered the better part of three years, from the time the Franklin Expedition left England to the time that Captain Crozier buried it in the ground. He'd made hundreds and hundreds of entries, but Major Hibble, the naval historian, confined his reading to the dozen or so entries that seemed to say it all:

19th May, 1845: We departed this day from London in search of the Northwest Passage. We are confident of achieving our goal because of certain advancements in human knowledge which have been made in these Enlightened Times. The *Erebus,* captained by Mr. Fitzjames, and the *Terror,* captained by yours truly, have mechanical engines to supplement the power of the wind. The hulls are reinforced with wooden beams and iron plates so they will not be crushed if we become marooned in the Pack Ice, as has happened on previous voyages of arctic discovery. To combat the pernicious effects of the Scurvy, we have assembled large barrels full of lime and lemon juice and are trying a new method of preserving meat in tins. This advance promises to make table both healthier and more pleasant for all, especially the officers. We also may benefit by the experience of Commander John Ross, whose men survived the arctic for three long winters without a single instance of the Scurvy. They accomplished this by consuming the raw flesh of seals and walrus, as the Savage Esquimaux are known to do. Naturally, we all to a man wish to avoid such an uncouth remedy to any nutritional problems we might encounter. Otherwise, our Expedition of Discovery is provisioned for a journey of three years with salt pork, chocolate, and concentrated soup. We also have a quantity of horseradish and cranberries. We are taking along a mechanical organ to protect the spirits of the men from the Melancholy which becomes epidemic during the long, cold arctic night. I am also informed that we will be experimenting with a French method of taking "Sun Pictures," a very modern art which we English have come to call Fotography. Our number is 129 of the best sailors in the British Empire. The foremost of these is Sir John Franklin, who knows the arctic well. Although he is of advanced age, he seems to possess a robust constitution. One might even call him fat were he not our leader and an honored peer known to all as the Polar Knight.

20th July, 1845: On this day in Baffin Bay we encountered the whaling ship *Prince of Wales,* which was headed back to Merrie England. As these were the last white men we may see for quite a while, we burdened them with letters of true devotion to our loved ones at home. Our plan is to make haste through Lancaster Sound so that we may attempt a few cursory Explorations before the freeze sets in and we are forced to call a temporary halt to our Discoveries.

15th September, 1845: After consulting with myself and the other officers, it was decided by Sir John that the continuance of hostile climatic conditions requires that we set up winter camp. We have chosen Beechey Island to be our temporary home. Those of the men who are new to the arctic are somewhat agitated by the prospect of spending many months in the place, but there is no logical alternative. Among the various terrors to be encountered, none has a more unsettling effect on the men than the realization that the months' long arctic night will soon be upon us. Captain Fitzjames, who excels in the manipulation of Numbers, calculates that the sun will set on 11th November and not rise again until 19th January.

6th January, 1846: A most disturbing situation has developed as concerns the Tinned Meat which was to provide us additional protection against the Scurvy. Early this morning, before the men were awake, the purser summoned Sir John and his senior officers so that we might surreptitiously inspect these provisions. We proceeded with the purser, Osmer is his name, to a hidden place behind the storehouse where he had arranged a large supply of Tinned Meat. Osmer selected one of these tins and placed it beneath Sir John's nose, bidding him smell it. The sour expression which came across our leader's face announced to us the discouraging news that the precious meat had spoiled. We counted as ruined 600 tins of 4 pounds each. We took a sun picture of the Tainted Meat for use in legal proceedings against the suppliers of this Voyage. However, we chose not to circulate this information among the men for fear that it would aggravate the Melan-

choly already caused among them by this Night
That Never Ends.

The naval historian stopped reading for a moment,
so that his audience could contemplate the unfolding
tragedy. He wiped his glasses with a handkerchief and
mumbled something to himself. Maybe it was a prayer
for Sir John and his men, and maybe it was something
else. He cleared his throat and read the following:

4th August, 1846: Cracks have opened in the ice
wall which has imprisoned us for ten months
now. We sail from Beechey Island tomorrow. Our
numbers are now 126, as we leave behind the last
remains of three stout fellows who perished from
various maladies. One was tubercular. Another
suffered the Deadly Chill. The third man died
from uncertain causes. Sir John believes that
Tinned Meat was an important element of this
last fatality, and said as much at burial services
held one day last week. He informed us that the
provisions were provided to us by Goldner and
Company, a thrifty London firm. He bade us
deny them our patronage should we ever have the
chance to do so.
12th September, 1846: On this day we were
beset by a series of singularly unfortunate circumstances that threaten the well-being of this Expedition. The men look to us for the consolation
provided by Informed Opinion, but must settle
for our mere pretense of same. The truth is, none
of the senior officers can explain the events that
transpired today, other than to say that we are
severely beset by Pack Ice, an observation which
the men can surely make for themselves. This
happened when we reached a narrows where the
sea is squeezed among four land masses: the

Boothia Peninsula, Prince of Wales Land, Victoria Land, and King William Land. It was at this juncture that great chunks of Ice became jammed together at the very moment we were attempting our passage. Captain Fitzjames believes that the large number of Ice Bergs which bedevil us are pieces of the Great Ice Wall that have broken off and drifted south. I would not presume to question his authority on this particular subject. It matters not one bit, because for whatever reason here we are and here we will stay until another Winter passes and the Pack Ice melts. I could not bear the thought of another Night That Never Ends, except for the fact that I must. Sir John is himself of a gloomy disposition, as this only compounds the worry caused in him by the Tinned Meat episode. Captain Fitzjames and I have ordered our men to perform vigorous exercises on the maindeck so that they will not be beset by Melancholy as well as Ice.

11th June, 1847: Sir John Franklin died today. His last breath was used to curse his enemies in Australia, although there were surely more immediate causes of his discomfort. Prior to his demise, he summoned me to his cabin for a private conversation. At this time he bade me deliver his last remains to the nearest point of land, so that he might have a good Christian burial. He wishes to be buried with certain properties which he deems to be of great value and importance. If I am able to discharge this commission and make safe passage through the Pack Ice, I am then to converse with one Maggie Stubbs, an Australian woman of easy virtue. I am to tell her that the Polar Knight was very brave but very poor, and inform her that there . . .

* * *

It was at this point that the reading was interrupted by a commotion. The Australian thieves were beside themselves at the news that Sir John died poor, while the Australian scientists became very excited for reasons of their own. All along they had believed that Sir John Franklin had been buried at sea. The naval historian took note of this, and then went on with his reading:

. . . and inform her that there is very little in his possession that is not the property of either Queen Victoria or Lady Jane Franklin, neither of whom can be counted on to make reparation for his youthful indiscretions. But beyond that this Miss Stubbs is to possess all that Sir John owns. I, of course, promised to discharge this commission, even though my chances of survival seem little better than his.

18th June, 1847: Lt. Gore has returned from the burial detail. He reports to me that his travel over the Pack Ice was uneventful despite the regular attention to his party of a very large Polar Bears, which he kept at bay by means of repeated rifle shots. He buried Sir John in frozen earth on the North West end of King William Land, which is seven miles from where we are beset. He conversed with the Esquimaux and marked Sir John's last resting place with a pile of stones and a message carved as follows on a piece of lumber taken from the HMS *Terror:* "Here lay the last remains of Sir John Franklin. Many died looking for the Northwest Passage. He died finding it on 11th June, 1847."

21st April, 1848: We will abandon ship tomorrow. I am not hopeful of our chances, but can see no other way. I have killed a small seal and am eating its uncooked flesh, in the manner of the

Esquimaux. The men prefer Beef Jerky and Tinned Meat, despite my warnings about its harmful effects upon the brain. Our plan of escape is an exceedingly desperate one. We will arrange the longboats on sleds and fill them with food and various trinkets that might be of such interest to the Esquimaux that they can be exchanged for a portion of healthy food. It seems a hopeless venture, but the wisest among us gave up hope many months ago, when the first spring came and still the Pack Ice did not melt. To my customary burdens of command are added the sad message that Sir John asked me to deliver to the Antipodes. This message burdens my heart and is of no use to starving men. But I promised to deliver it if I could, and I intend to discharge that commission with sufficient zeal should circumstance allow me to do so.

25th April, 1848: We made land today and called it Victory Point. We are on the western coast of King William Land, near where Lt. Gore said he buried Sir John Franklin. I was hoping to say a prayer for the Polar Knight, but the rocks that were used to mark his grave have been scattered by the terrible action of the Pack Ice as it grinds against the land. I can report that we are in the vicinity of a great number of Walrus. I killed one of these sea cows before it could go into the sea. We all had a portion of meat, but most of the men refused to eat it raw, to the detriment of their physical condition, which is very much in need of improvement. There are 105 Souls still alive among us, but half of these are half dead already.

1st August, 1848: This day we encountered a group of Esquimaux, who gave us a small seal in exchange for an elegant table setting. They have no table, of course. I suspect this bargain has more to do with pity or fear than self-interest, and will be surprised if they want to carry on additional exchanges of this sort. The Esquimaux call me Aglooka for some reason that I cannot ascertain. It seems that these Savages have a certain regard for me, although I cannot explain why they should. The thought occurs that it might be wise to cast my lot with them. I would do so immediately were it not for the burden of leadership that rests upon my shoulders. Without their help, we are surely doomed. Of the 5 Souls now living, only I have avoided the Scurvy thanks to . . .

"That'll do, Major Hibble," Dr. Godwin said.

She was going to say something else, something sentimental and profound. But before she could another notion intruded. She looked around with increasing anxiety until her gaze stopped at me. "Where's Frankie?" she said.

I told her I didn't know. Then I told her that he and Donald left after the part where they buried Sir John at Victory Point.

"That little bastard," she said to me. To the scientists she said, "We better move fast, lads, or they'll beat us to the goods—I mean the artifacts."

CHAPTER 20

Dr. Godwin had changed her mind about me. At first she wanted me out of her sight. Now she wanted to keep an eye on me, for reasons I didn't understand. The two of us rode with Dr. Bud in the cab of the tractor-trailer. Gravel crunched beneath the wheels as Bud guided the Vibroseise Device around the pingos and polygons that pressed against the beach on the north coast of King Will's Island.

The north coast was a lot like the east coast and the south coast. We were traveling counterclockwise along a sort of a circle that was made of gravel and ice. There was a chill in the air and the pack ice shifted as the tide rolled in. The sky was tinted an uncertain gray, as if it might rain, or it might snow, or it might do nothing at all.

"Winter's coming," Dr. Godwin said.

"How can you tell?" I replied.

"The tundra's changing color, going from green to brown. That means the plants are dying and winter will be here soon. Are you prepared for winter? I'm told that it gets very cold."

I had to confess that I wasn't prepared. She seemed pleased by this, as if it confirmed some long-cherished suspicion she had about men or broadcast journalists. I counterattacked: "So what were you and Frankie like as kids?"

Dr. Bud cleared his throat. He always does that when he's about to pay very close attention to something or other.

"We fought a lot over very little, as children so often do. He was very smart but he never studied. He preferred to go surfing with his worthless friends. Surfing is a most despicable sport, a dangerous way of wasting time. I believe you Americans invented it. It's very popular in Oz, which is surrounded by waves, of course. Be that as it may, Franklin never achieved his potential, while I've already exceeded mine. That's the way it is, Mr. Riordan. Do you often pry into family affairs?"

"Only when there's a chance I can make some money at it. That story I was telling you about. I think I'll start out with the legend of Maggie Stubbs."

The chill in the air did not come from the iceberg sea, or the northerly wind that was killing the plants. It came from a look so full of hate that Dr. Bud was required to clear his throat a second time.

"That would be a big mistake, Mr. Riordan. I plan to write that one myself for a very handsome sum. If you print a word about Maggie Stubbs I'll sue you for everything you've got."

Bud tried not to laugh, but he couldn't help himself. As the mirth came out in pressurized guffaws, he pretended that he was coughing. Dr. Godwin was not deceived.

"What seems to be the problem, Bud?"

He laughed so hard he cried, and almost ran into a pingo. He took a moment to catch his breath. "I'm sorry, Bev, but you cracked me up. If you sued Pres for all he's got, all you'd get is a couple of celebrity posters and a dog so old she can hardly stand up by herself. Pres doesn't even have a place of his own. He sleeps in back of the radio station."

Dr. Godwin didn't move, blink, or say a thing. Her jaw turned white, her cheeks turned red and she looked at something very far away. Her version of the thousand-yard stare was different in one important respect: She was really looking at something. After a while she told us what it was.

"Night's coming, lads. I hope you're well prepared. Night's like winter, only worse. Or at least that's what I've been told."

Sure enough we could see a black band of darkness gathering over the southern sky. We hadn't seen a real night since spring came to the Bodenburg Butte. Dusk went right into dawn in that part of the world at that time of the year.

"It's amazing how fast it happens," Dr. Godwin said. "We'll have about ten minutes of dark tonight and twenty minutes tomorrow. Three hours by next Monday and nine hours the Monday after that. The nights are terribly cold, of course. I hope you've packed your snuggies."

We camped for the night at Cape Felix, an elbow of land about ten miles shy of Victory Point. I wondered who Felix was and what he had done to earn such a dubious honor. Dr. Bud smuggled me some leftovers from the Spartan dinner the scientists had: a few pieces of bread smeared with a bland paste called

Vegemite, a failed Australian attempt to improve on peanut butter. My friend was already sound asleep by the time I'd forced these victuals down. I decided to stay up a bit and see if Dr. Godwin had been right about the night.

Sure enough, the black band in the southern sky spread like a pestilence until it covered King Will's Island. There were about ten minutes of pitch-black between the dark grays of dusk and dawn. I crawled into Dr. Bud's tent and slept but did not rest.

If death was a sensation, instead of just a destiny, I think it would feel like I felt during our mad rush to Victory Point. The night had brought along a chill and had left a fog behind. This ice fog smelled like winter and tasted like the salt sea from which it had emerged. It drenched our clothes and confused our senses, as if the thick soup had seeped into our brains.

Even so, we continued our journey westward along the northern coast of the island. We could only travel as fast as a man could walk, the man being Dr. Bud, who scouted the terrain up ahead for pingos, polygons, and other obstacles which might do damage to the Vibroseise Device. The photogrammarian took the wheel of the tractor-trailer, but we didn't talk much as he needed to concentrate on Dr. Bud's constant instructions:

"Pingo at twelve o'clock. Try a little more brake and give me a ten-degree turn to the right."

Or, "We've got a small crack in the ground about ten yards up ahead. When I say 'Go!' you give it a little extra gas and that'll get you over the crack without getting your wheels stuck."

Or, "Brakes! Brakes! Give me brakes!"

The wind shifted in the early afternoon, and the ice

fog started to drift back into the sea from which it came. We occasionally rolled into clear pockets from which we could see the pack ice on our right and the permafrost on our left. These pockets became more frequent until we broke into the clear.

Dr. Bud took the wheel and we started to make some time. The icebergs seemed much larger now, and their progress had slowed to a crawl. The pack ice was getting bigger and starting to move our way. The colder it got, the faster we moved, until we arrived at Victory Point.

Victory Point looked and sounded like a punch into the belly of the Great Ice Pack. It was wedged between two towering walls of ice and produced a tremendous animal noise that said it all at once: food, shelter, sleep, love, hate, and fear. The far tip of the place was home to a herd of fat organ grinders with flippers and oversize vampire teeth. The mammalian biologist identified these as a herd of *Odobenus obesus*.

He said, "The Vikings called it the whale horse and the Beatles called it the walrus."

Inland was something I hadn't expected: a large mobile home sitting on top of a pingo. We couldn't see who lived there, but I assumed that they could see us and probably disapproved. The owners of the mobile home couldn't be too far away because the pingo it was on was surrounded by dozens of noisy dogs. On the perimeter were polar bear dogs. Out alone with no protection, these scrawny, wolfish beasts strained against their chains and watched the pack ice with deep interest. Closer to the pingo, sled dogs were huddled together, sometimes playing but mostly sleeping as they waited for their next assignment.

The Australian thieves had set up camp about a half mile down the beach. They had reinforcements and fresh supplies, the results, I assume, of an airlift by the Canadian pilot. The pilot was nowhere to be seen, but the Gripper was back among us. He glared at me when Dr. Godwin dragged me along on a visit to her brother.

She said, "What are you doing, you little twit?"

Frankie appeared to be poking around in the tundra, looking around in the listless way of a man searching for something he doesn't expect to find. "I'm looking for our dear dead ancestor, sis. What I want to do is dig him up, pick his pockets, and then give him a proper burial. Maybe get a headstone and all. I want it to read: 'Here lies the frozen Franklin, buried in ice until the end of time.' Quite spiffy, don't you think? It'll give the tourists a tingle."

"And why are you digging here?"

"Why not? It's as good a place as any. Besides, I figure that digging in the dirt is really your job, since you're the one with the college degree."

The other thieves started to snicker. They stopped as soon as Dr. Godwin looked their way. Frankie shrugged and went back to digging his hole. It gave him something to do while the Vibroseise Device pounded away at Victory Point.

We took turns standing next to the machine, feeling its vibrations course through our bodies. It pounded the ground for a week, but didn't find a thing. No body, no goods; not even a piece of silverware. The closest they came was early Wednesday, when the geologist from Petco picked up an unusual reading. "Whatever it is, it's big," he said. "And I mean really big. Is it true Sir John was fat when he died?"

The naval historian nodded. This was his area of expertise. He'd written a paper on the ratio of protein to fat in military food. The geologist thought before he spoke again. "Well, it could be him if he was really, really fat."

They unpacked the thermal bore. It churned the beach into rubble and created so much excitement that the people who lived in the mobile home finally showed themselves. It was an elderly Eskimo couple dressed in furs and bunny boots. The man was bow-legged and fat, built like a figure 8. His wife spoke Inupiat and he spoke English. They wanted to know what was going on.

"My woman very much enjoys your big amazing machines," the old man said to no one in particular. "She likes the one that shakes the beach and makes her feel like mating. Now you have this new machine that sets the beach on fire."

The geologist turned off the thermal bore. The steam rose into the clouds, leaving behind a hole in the beach. Dr. Godwin spoke to the Eskimos. "You can see that the beach is not on fire. We're only digging a hole. Come here and see for yourself."

The old couple talked it over in their own language before deciding to agree. The geologist gave them a demonstration of how to use a thermal bore. It generated a great cloud of steam to soften the perma-frost, and then used a heated bit to drill a hole in the ground. They dug deeper into the permafrost, but all they found were the fossilized bones of a prehistoric walrus. The scientists were disappointed. The Eskimo couple was not impressed.

The old man said, "You people should not torment the dead. Let this walrus rest in peace."

Most of the scientists were ready to do just that, but the mammalian biologist was not among them. He knew a lot about dead animals and he hoped that this one might produce a scholarly paper for his collection, perhaps something on the subject of the arctic food chain.

"If I had to guess, I would say that this *Odobenus obesus* was killed by a group of Eskimos. See how some of the bones were broken in half. Eskimos break the bones so they can suck the marrow out. A polar bear would never do that. A dog or a wolf might try but they could never break bones as big as that."

His lecture lost its urgency as soon as he noticed that Dr. Godwin wasn't paying attention. She was talking to the couple with breathless urgency about ancient stories she had heard. Frankie and Donald returned to their camp and the other scientists drifted back to their own experiments. The Gripper was the only person who took much interest in the walrus bones. He was concerned with everything that had to do with food.

August became September and the icebergs slowed to a stop. They pounded the ground for three more days without finding a thing. Each day was colder and each night was longer. All work came to a halt on the fourth day, which brought a snowstorm that blew harder and harder without exhausting itself. The snow turned the island so white we couldn't tell where the island ended and the pack ice began. We crowded into a large, heated tent that the scientists used when they wanted to attend to their specimens. Most of the team paid no attention to me as they fussed with their precious artifacts. I was just another curiosity, something they'd found under a rock that might be of interest some day.

The botanist showed me the newest edition to his

plant collection. It looked like a mushroom gone to mold. "I've been thinking lately," he said. "Maybe I'll write a paper for the *London Botanical Report*. Those pommies'll eat it up."

"What's a pommie?" I inquired.

The botanist was delighted that I'd asked. "Pommies're Englishmen, heroic explorers of the Great Indoors. They're either very fat or very skinny and they almost never get a tan. When somebody calls you a pommie bastard consider yourself insulted, you pommie bastard."

I laughed. He didn't. I think he was beginning to suspect that I wasn't going to feature him in the story I had promised to write. I was watching the botanist tend to his tundra plants when we heard a peculiar cry.

"Coo-eee! Coo-eee!"

It was the mammalian biologist. The botanist and I rushed down to the beach and saw that he was pointing at the pack ice, at the place where the walrus were sunning themselves.

"Polar bear," the biologist said.

"Where?"

"Right over there."

All I could see were the walrus, flapping their flippers in the breeze. Then one of the smaller walrus screamed and a polar bear came out of nowhere as if it was made of the snow itself. The bear tore open its victim's throat with a short, strong swipe of its paw. The other walrus had already retreated, except for the great gray bull. He made a noise that sounded like a pig might sound if a pig was as big as a house, then slipped into the water after his frightened harem. Blood turned the pack ice pink.

Most of us started to shuffle away, our eyes all lowered by that grateful guilt that survivors so often feel. The TV photographer stifled a cheer. He'd caught it all on film and thought it would make a great segment on "Science Today."

The TV writer wasn't so sure. "We can't show that on public television. We'd lose ten thousand subscribers."

The producer had a compromise. "Well, we won't show it during pledge week, and we can cut out all the bloody parts."

The photographer disagreed. "There are no parts if we cut out the blood. Everything else looks like a snowflake in a blizzard."

The producer was clearly in a quandary. His way of dealing with quandaries was to pace in a circle with his hands clasped behind his back, like Groucho Marx without the jokes. Finally he decided not to decide. None of his people seemed too surprised.

The producer had other things on his mind besides what to do with the polar bear film. He was worried about the weather and thought he might have to pull the plug and start heading back to Boston. "We're running out of light," he said. "We can't shoot film in the dark."

Dr. Godwin smiled that special smile that every man thinks is just for him. "I understand completely, but let's give it another week. We've still got plenty of light, you know, and there's still one place we haven't checked."

"What place is that?" the producer asked.

She replied, "The best place of all. Under the old people's house."

* * *

Dr. Godwin led a delegation to the only part of Victory Point that hadn't been Vibroseised.

The old man spoke in a stoic monotone. "My family has lived here for more than a hundred years. And now you ask us to move our house? This is a serious matter. I must discuss this with my wife."

They spoke Inupiat for several minutes, then started to smile and nod their heads. I thought I heard some scientists expel a collective sigh, the sound of answered prayers. The old man said, "White people are very strange. Why must you haunt the dead? First you torment the walrus and now you torment the man."

The scientists who'd sighed before now decided to hold their breath. This was it. It had to be.

"I don't understand," Dr. Godwin said, but she said it in a way that made me think that she did.

The elder couple grunted and squeaked. Then the man translated. "This is why you won't let the dogs eat the meat of dead people? So you can come back later and haunt their restless spirits?"

Dr. Godwin paced back and forth at the foot of the pingo. The rest of us were content to watch, especially her beloved photogrammarian. She wore tight fatigues and combat boots and looked well scrubbed despite the fact that fresh water was in short supply.

She said, "Tell me a story about this place and how you came to live here. I am a woman who listens. Isn't that what every man wants?"

The old man translated this for his wife, who thought about it for a moment, then laughed so hard she almost fell down. She said something in Inupiat which her husband repeated in English. "My wife says that every man wants a woman who listens, and every woman wants a man who talks but nobody ever gets what they want. I will now tell you the story of our house."

He danced while he talked, and used extravagant gestures to propel the tale.

"My father said that in the second winter after Big Kayaks With Wings got stuck in the ice long ago, some white men came here with a dead friend who was fatter than an Eskimo. They dug a big hole in the world and put the dead man in it. The Old Ones thought this was very strange and asked the white man called Lieutenant Gore why this was necessary. The Old Ones said, 'Give this meat to our dogs. They work hard and are very hungry.' But Lieutenant Gore replied, 'Englishmen don't do that. We believe in eternal life.'

"The Old Ones smiled at this, and made a joke among themselves. 'What good is this eternal life if you must spend it buried forever in the frozen world? It must be very dull. We believe it is better to give your meat to the dogs. They need meat. Winter is coming soon.'

"Lieutenant Gore was made to sweat by this conversation. It's very strange the way white men waste valuable heat in this way. He made the Old Ones promise not to dig up the dead white man and give his meat to their dogs. The Old Ones promised to do this, and Lieutenant Gore gave them many useless things as a sign of his appreciation. These useless things were left as a gift to the Great Ice Pack, but the Old Ones kept their promise and made their children keep this promise too. Even to this day, the dead man is trapped down there in a wooden box surrounded by rocks. That's why we build our house there. It makes a very solid foundation. So tell us this now: If we let you dig him up, can our dogs have his meat to eat?"

Dr. Godwin said, "No. I can't do that. We still believe in eternal life, although sometimes I have my doubts. Ask me for something else and I'll give it to you if I can."

The old man smiled without any teeth. "I will let you move this house if you give my wife a gift."

Now it was Dr. Godwin's turn to smile. She said, "Certainly. What would you suggest?"

Husband and wife talked things over in Inupiat. They smiled a lot and laughed when they were finished. The old man said, "My wife would like to borrow your Vibroseise Device. She says it makes her body tingle and causes me to act like a young hunter in love. This is a remarkable thing for a man with seventeen children and so many grandchildren that I don't even count anymore. It makes my wife so happy that she doesn't even talk as much. This Vibroseise Device will bring me love and peace. What more could an old man want?"

They loaded the mobile home onto the tractor-trailer, hauled it down to the western beach, and set it down next to the Vibroseise Device. Dr. Bud showed them how to turn it on and off. I said, "All in the name of science, right?"

Bud was worried about something. I asked him what it was. He said, "I'm worried about Petco. If they put this part on 'Science Today,' Petco's not going to like it. They're supposed to be used for science, not as a marital aide."

Bud sidled over to where the TV producer was in eager conference with his writer, photographer, and sound man. I sidled over too and heard what they had to say:

   Writer: "I think we could say a lot without saying anything. We show a picture of the machine with some crisp natural sound of the heavy buzz it makes. Cut to a shot of the couple looking happy and walking into their mobile home. The narrator says something indirect about it. Something like 'The Eskimo inhabitants of the area are amazed by western technology.' Or something along those lines. I'll write it later when we see what fits."
   Sound Man: "I've got natural sound of the Vibroseise buzz."
   Photographer: "And I've got this shot where the couple gets the giggles, when they were talking about it in Eskimo."
   Producer: "Perfect. We can even mention Petco again and maybe they'll give us a corporate grant."

"Science Today" asked the botanist to explain what a pingo is. The botanist was thrilled, of course. The "Science Today" photographer walked backward in front of the scientist as he expelled clouds of hot, moist wisdom into the frosted day.

"It's a Canadian word, I'm afraid. You know, there's really not a lot of those. It's a conical hill caused by the action of the frost. What we have here is a tundra bog that's frozen most of the time. This causes the ground to expand upward on a verticle plane. Bingo! You've got a pingo. Like a pimple on the face of the earth."

"Cut!" the TV producer said. "We've got a good sound bite here."

"But what about my cactus project?" the intrepid botanist said. "I can't write a paper on pingos. I'm afraid it's been done before."

The thieves watched with interest as the scientists used great clouds of steam to thaw the frozen hill. It was mostly gravel underneath a thin layer of dead plants and topsoil. The bigger rocks were photographed and entered on a chart so that they could be returned to their proper places when the excavation was completed.

Dr. Godwin said, "Under the authority vested in me by Permit Number 31490HRC issued by the Franklin District of the Northwest Territories, I declare this to be an Official Archeological Site and as such protected by the laws of England and the Dominion of Canada."

"Bullshit!" her brother said. "That's a lot of twaddle. You just want to hog it all for yourself."

CHAPTER 21

The body of Sir John Franklin, if that's who it really was, was buried in a cairn. *Cairn* is a Scottish word for the Scottish notion that rocks could be piled on top of each other to make a signal of sorts. The botanist and the geologist conspired to inform us just how Sir John's burial cairn came to be covered by a pingo.

According to the geologist, "The seasonal advance of the ice pack would have covered the cairn with dirt and silt that would be left behind in the summer, when the ice pack retreated into the sea."

The botanist agreed because dirt and silt mean plants, and plants were his specialty. "Of course, the indigenous flora grows wherever there's dirt and silt. It's an aggressive sort of vegetation, the plant that's most like an animal. If they buried Sir John in 1847, he could have been covered with flowers twelve months later. No wonder they never found the cairn. It looked like a typical pingo."

Fortunately for the public record, the Eskimo man

happened by. He said, "I really like your story and will tell it to all my children. But you might want to know the truth about this cairn that looks like a pingo. The truth is the Old Ones were offended by this stone place the white men built so that they could haunt the dead. So the Old Ones covered the stone place with dirt they scraped from the ground so the summertime plants would grow. It is much better to look at than a stone igloo with dead meat in it."

The geologist was discouraged by this and the botanist was indifferent. But the naval historian was beside himself with joy. "Of course," he gloated. "This explains everything. I'll write a paper about it. There were dozens of ships from all over the world that came here looking for Sir John. But they never found his burial place. That's why they figured he'd been buried at sea. Heroes from many countries came here looking for Sir John Franklin. Captain Rasmusson of Sweden, and Sir Leopold McClintock, of course. Then there was this American chap named Hall. He was some sort of religious fanatic from your Cincinnati, Ohio. But none of them found the Polar Knight because they were all looking for a cairn when they should have been looking for a pingo. Thank God for the Vibroseise Device!"

"You've got that right," the Eskimo said. "I feel like I'm young again. Every old man should have one."

It's a funny thing about scientists, at least Australian ones. The more excited they get, the more slowly they move. They dismantled the cairn stone by stone until a plain wooden box was exposed. The box was implanted in the permafrost, so they had a long discussion about what to do next: remove the box from the permafrost, or open the box and remove the body.

The naval historian wanted to remove the box. Perhaps it was made from pieces of a ship. Tests would have to be conducted and papers would have to be written.

Dr. Godwin disagreed. "We don't want to disturb the site any more than we have to. Let's open it up and lift him out."

The permafrost had preserved his every feature for a hundred and forty-three years. He was a fat man with a large head and big brown eyes. He had no hair on top, but plenty on the sides. His blue lips were peeled away from a grotesque smile, like that given to the gargoyles in the darkest part of a cathedral. His face was a sickly color, mostly green and yellow, but his gums were a healthy pink and he had more teeth than the Gripper. He wore a dark blue naval uniform with buttons on his cuffs and medals. With the death grip of his chubby hands he clutched to his chest copperplates tinted with shades of gray.

"Sun pictures!" the photogrammarian exclaimed. "Now I can write a paper too!"

Several scientists shook his hand and toasted his good fortune with a round of foaming frosties. Then we all filed into the laboratory where the corpse was laid on a table formerly devoted to the botanist's plant collection. Counting thieves, scholars, and TV people, there must have been twenty people in that tent. We filled the place with body steam.

"I'm afraid you'll have to get out," Dr. Godwin said.

"Why's that, sis?" her brother replied.

"It's getting too hot in here. We mustn't let the specimen thaw or it's sure to decompose."

"I just want the goods is all. You can keep the stiff."

"Well, you're not getting any 'goods' so just get out of here." She turned to the photogrammarian. "Kinsley . . .".

Her lover had fetched an enormous elephant gun, which he now pointed at Frankie. The young thief didn't seem alarmed by this.

"Right, sis," Frankie said. "We're on the move right now."

This called for another round of foaming frosties. Dr. Bud let me have a sip of his. The sun was starting to disappear and the wind was picking up speed. The photogrammarian sucked in cold air and blew out hot.

"I guess I showed that little punk," he announced to an eager audience. "I can't say as I blame him, though. Those pictures're worth a bundle. There's collectors that'll pay millions and museums'll pay even more."

I said, "Frankie's got a letter that says they're his—or at least that's what he says it says."

Kinsley was ready for this one. "Is it a will that's duly notarized and prepared by a licensed barrister? Does it mention anything about photographs or 'sun pictures' if you will? Can he prove that the letter is authentic? Does it have the force of law? Or is it just an elaborate caper cooked up by a gang of convicted felons?"

I shrugged my shoulders and dropped the subject. Kinsley seemed pleased with himself, so pleased that he launched into a lengthy lecture on the subject of photogrammetics. The other scientists had to listen.

"Of course, I haven't had a real close look, but the

one sun picture that we can see—the one on top of the stack—looks like it might be of some sort of flag-planting ceremony. You can see the old Union Jack and somebody standing next to it, but you can't see who's holding the flag. Sir John's thumb is in the way. But let's say just that it is what it appears to be. I'll be able to tell exactly when and where that picture was taken. First I measure the shadows, of course, and compute their angle as relates to the horizon. There's this formula we use to plug the numbers in and bingo! bango! there you have it: the date, time, and place that the photograph was taken. This is a new branch of science and I'm on the cutting edge. This'll keep me in grants until I retire. Life is good, mates. There is no doubt about that. Now, if you'll excuse me, it's time to tuck it in. Has anyone seen Beverly about?"

The group congratulated Kinsley, who then went off in search of his beloved. The other scientists broke into smaller groups to talk about the various possibilities. One of the things that scientists do is pretend an interest in one another's work. It's a boring job, but somebody's got to do it. The naval historians commented on the condition of Sir John's uniform while the botanist wondered aloud to Dr. Bud whether there might not be some sort of arctic fungus growing on the corpse. The mammalian biologist talked about the mint condition of the specimen while the toxicologist speculated on what new information an autopsy might disclose.

That was about all the science I could take, so I wandered down to the beach to watch the sun go down. The Vibroseise Device was still and the home of the elderly Eskimos was quiet and dark at last. I wondered if their many children visited them in this lonely place. Did they laugh and sing and tell old stories?

"Hello, sport," the Gripper said.

I almost jumped out of my shoes. I couldn't see him at first. He was hiding in a shadow that the pack ice caused where it crunched against the beach.

"Hello, Grip," I replied. I started to walk away but didn't get very far before he caught up with me and stuck a handgun in my ribs. When I tried to get away, he grabbed the lobe of my left ear and used it to tug me along. He almost tore it off when I stumbled over a rock. He took me behind a pingo and threw me to the ground, which was cold, wet, and as hard as marble. I looked up to see Donald and Frankie standing there. Frankie looked sad. Donald looked annoyed.

"What's going on?" I said.

"Shut up, twit," Donald replied. Then he turned to Frankie and said, "Here's the what's what, as far as I can see. Your sister is playing a game with us. She'll never give up the goods. I say we grab what we come for and then fly on out of here. I don't want to hear about the laws of England and Canada. We all live in Oz and we've got this letter here to show that the goods belong to us."

Frankie nodded slowly, although it wasn't clear whether he was agreeing with what Donald said or nodding about something else. Donald said, "The first thing we do is snuff this donger and bury him in the snow someplace."

Donald was looking right at me. The Gripper became visibly excited. Frankie thought about it.

"Wait a second," I said. "Why do you want to do that? I don't want your goods. I just want to go home."

Donald said, "Home to your radio station, right?

The problem with you is you know too much and you're a bleeding celebrity. I don't want you talking about the Ned Kelly Gang on your radio show back home. You radio people are always flapping jaw, and the gang don't like publicity. It interferes with business."

"Right, Donnie," Frankie said. "But I wouldn't do it here. Some dog'll come along and dig up his body and somebody'll find the bones. There'll be an investigation and they'll be sure to pin it on us. I think we'd be better off if we threw him out of the plane."

Donald nodded and the Gripper pounced on me. I made the mistake of putting up a fight. He ended my resistance with a powerful jab to the side of my head. Night fell quicker than it ever fell before, and winter started right away.

The Cessna still smelled like meat and its floor was still stained with blood of the hunt. Before I came to my senses, I had a vivid dream about the people who'd used this plane before. They were big and strong and had the All-Alaska look: bunny boots, green fatigues, heavy beards, and lumberjack shirts. They tracked down a bull moose and killed it with a single shot and drank too much beer as they butchered their kill in the field. Afterward they ate some moose and told each other stories that everybody enjoyed but nobody believed.

One of the dream stories was about a hunt that wouldn't end for a moose that wouldn't die no matter how many times they shot it. The smell of blood became so thick that I started to croak and gag. That's when I came to my senses. I was crammed among some bundles that were packed into the tail of the plane. On them were stitched the simple legend: PARA-

CHUTE SURVIVE PAK PROPERTY OF THE ALASKA NATIONAL GUARD.

Someone snickered. It was the pilot. He was at the controls, but the plane was still on the ground. I asked him where the Australians were, but he didn't want to say. I nodded at the bundles in a hopeful way. He said, "We borrowed those Survive Paks from the Herc those Aussie scientists are using. We're getting low on supplies and in case you haven't noticed, this is a difficult place. It's best to be prepared for just about anything."

"My head hurts," I said.

He smiled as if he cared. "I never let the Gripper get too close to me. He's crazy, you know. You can tell if you watch him real close. He spends a lot of time staring at things that aren't there and sometimes he talks to himself when he thinks that nobody's looking, eh? The Gripper's going to explode someday. Guys like that always do. I don't want to be around him when it happens."

I tried to sit up but it made me feel dizzy. I lay back down on the floor. "You keep a pretty low profile."

"It's the secret of my success. My father was a very smart man. Do you know what he said to me one time? I was about ten and he took me to the Toronto Zoo. It was springtime and all the animals were trying to screw, even the polar bears. My father was hoping I would get the picture so he wouldn't have to tell me the facts of life. I got the picture but made him tell me anyway. He squirmed like a polar bear in heat. That was my father, eh? You know what he said to me one time?"

"What?"

"He said, 'Son, God gave you two ears and one mouth. Use them in that proportion and everything will be okay.' My father was wrong about a lot of things, but I think he was right about that. I don't talk very much. It's made me a wealthy man. That's your problem. You talk too much. What's it like to be on the radio?"

"It's like nothing," I replied. "Radio people live on the air and they don't have any bodies. Ugly guys work on the radio, but they meet a lot of women anyway because the women who listen to radio think radio people look like their voices sound: big, deep, rich . . ."

He wasn't listening anymore, but staring at something off in the distance. It was dark and cold outside. When a light flashed three times, the pilot flipped a switch and the engine coughed to life. The propellers made a blizzard in the snow.

After three more flashes, he released the brake. My head still hurt but I sat up anyway. We were taxiing down the beach, toward the big green field tent that the scientists used as their laboratory. When we reached it the tent flapped open and the thieves charged out with something heavy wrapped in cloth. Donald fired a gun in the air as Frankie and the Gripper loaded their burden into the plane. It was the still-frozen body of Sir John Franklin. A few seconds later we were bouncing down the beach and up into the sky. We turned left and headed south, flying above the ice pack as it gathered off the western shore, bringing food and shelter to the polar bears and death to everything else.

CHAPTER 22

We climbed into the night, above dark clouds heavy with snow. The Canadian pilot asked the question that was most on my mind. I couldn't ask it because I was hoping they'd forget I was in the plane. The pilot said, "I don't mean to get involved in your business, eh, but why'd you steal the stiff?"

Donald and the Gripper gave Frankie an accusing look. The Gripper said, "Frankie here's been bit by the Jesus bug. He's all of a sudden got religion and wants to make sure that Gramps gets a proper burial."

Frankie said, "That's only part of it. The other part is we're not real sure about what we're looking for. We could have snatched the pictures, but maybe there's something else—like a deed to Donnie's shopping mall or stock in a secret gold mine."

Donald said, "Bulsh, Frankie. Bulsh. You heard what that Captain Crozier wrote. This old fella didn't even have a pot to piddle in. There's no deed to nothing."

"But we don't know that for sure. It could be that Captain Crozier was wrong. Or maybe Sir Johnny told them a story so's they wouldn't steal the goods."

The pilot nodded reluctantly. "Okay, eh. Whatever you say. So let's get on with it then, before he starts to melt."

The Gripper looked at me in an enthusiastic way. "What about the Radio Star?"

I wrapped my arms around a Parachute Survive Pak and held on for dear life. The Gripper knocked me loose with a quick kick between my shoulder blades. The pilot fiddled with one of his instruments and the plane's hum became less intense, like a car slipping into a faster gear. He shouted over the engine noise, "Take it easy there, Grip. I wouldn't do it right away. If you're sure you want to throw him out, we'll do it over open water. Otherwise he'll land on the beach or on the pack ice just offshore, and make a big red splat that the Mounties can see all the way from Fort Resolution. Then we'll all be facing life in a Canadian prison. You want to spend the rest of your life with a bunch of Canadians? Take it from me; you don't."

The Gripper let go of me. I dropped to the floor like a pile of laundry he didn't want to do. Donald started to pound his forehead with the palm of his left hand, as if that might somehow shake free the thought he was trying to think. After a while he said, "How long?"

The pilot checked his speedometer, then said, "We wait thirty minutes, maybe forty. We'll be hitting open water in Queen Maude's Gulf and then it won't be a problem. He'll sink like a rock with that metal leg he's got and the fishes'll eat him for dinner, eh?"

Donald managed to nod yes and shake no at the same time. He agreed with the pilot's thinking, but didn't like it much. He looked at Frankie, who was staring at Sir John. Donald said, "Well, you better check for the goods then, before he gets too ripe."

Sir John smiled at us with his sardonic grin and perfect teeth. The thieves had stolen him in the middle of some sort of scientific procedure. His coat and shirt had been unbuttoned to reveal a large, hairy chest and a larger, though less hairy, belly. His insides were trying to get out through a hole the size of a nickel that the pathologist had drilled into his frozen solar plexus.

Frankie said, "He died of a heart attack."

"How do you know that?" I said.

"I asked the guy that drilled that hole before we stole the stuff. They were doing an autopsy. He said it was a massive cardial infarction. I said, 'What's that?' He said, 'A heart attack.' He could have had a heart attack anywhere, back in London, even. I guess that's why they called him the Polar Knight, because he had to come up here to have a heart attack."

Donald said, "Sleep tight, Polar Knight. We're going to take a peak at your goods."

He didn't give up the pictures without a fight. Despite Frankie's protests, the Gripper had to saw off the tips of his thumbs with a serrated hunting knife before he could slip the photographs free. There were three of the copperplates. Tucked between two of them was a letter from Lady Jane Franklin to her intrepid husband. Frankie read the letter out loud:

My Dearest Sir John,
    I hope you enjoy your brand-new toy, and put it to proper use. The Frenchies call it daguerreo-typography and it's the very latest thing. Imagine

painting pictures with light. We live in a world of wonders, and you, my dear husband, are certain to accomplish one of them. I am sure in my heart that this time you will discover the Northwest Passage, although I'm less certain what our government will do with it once you've discovered it. The northern route seems to be a singularly unpleasant way to get to the Orient, but I am but a woman, and what do women know of such things? Our Dear Queen excepted, of course.

As to this Australian business, I strongly advise against a visit to the Antipodes. The Australians have not been kind to us, and I see no reason that we should be kind to them. The place has a back of steel and a heart of stone, and you're getting too old for that sort of thing. You'd be much better off heading due south and touring the United States. I've heard you're quite a hero there, especially in New York.

> Your beloved,
> Lady Jane

Frankie's hands were shaking. The sun pictures made that little thunder noise that thin sheets of metal produce when they are wobbled. The Gripper said to Frankie, "A couple of crummy photographs. I hope there's something in his pockets. If there ain't then we're as poor as Sir Johnny over there."

Donald said, "That's where you're wrong, Grip. I heard this photographer say that pictures like this'll be worth a lot of money if we can find a buyer. Sell them to the Japs, maybe. They've got all the greenies." He turned to Frankie. "Did you check his pockets yet?"

Frankie laid the pictures down. I crawled over to take a peek at the three plates smudged with shades of black and gray: Two ships stuck in the pack ice, three men standing near a British flag, triangle stacks of unmarked food cans such as you might find on display at the Hudson Bay Company Store. I did a quick calculation in my head based on stories I'd read in *People Magazine; Sun Pictures,* the book; *Sun Pictures,* the movie; "Sun Pictures," the television show. Then there were the pictures themselves. Frankie was a very rich thief.

"St. Paul's balls!" the Gripper said. "It's just a bunch of junk."

Frankie had his hands full of Sir John's belongings; a rusty knife, a pocket watch, and a medal from the British government. The medal was wrapped in a tattered handkerchief like a good-luck charm that didn't work.

"Get away from them pictures, sport," Frankie said to me.

The Gripper supported this with a snarl. I backed away. Frankie collected the pictures and laid them in a neat stack next to the things from Sir John's pockets. Donald said without much hope, "Try taking off his shoes. Maybe there's papers hidden there. Shoes is always a good hiding place."

The boot was frozen to the foot. "I'll have to cut it off," Frankie said. The Gripper suggested an ax, but Frankie used a saw instead, carefully cutting the sole away so as not to slice off too much foot. Some damage was unavoidable.

The first boot was empty, but the second contained a letter. "They sure wrote a lot of letters," the Gripper said.

Donald thought about it so hard he almost hurt himself. Finally he replied, "No telly back then. Nothing else to do."

Frankie read the letter out loud:

My Dearest Maggie,

I am near the end of my appointed time, and it's clear to me now that I will not discover a northern route to the Orient and neither will I make it to Australia, as I have promised you. Even at this last passage in my life, I dare not confess our shame to anyone. So I write you a letter that I cannot send about riches I do not have. The truth is, dear heart, I'm a poor but famous man. If only I could bequeath you my celebrity. You see, my father was a minister of God and I spent most of my life at sea, collecting accolades while smarter men were collecting gold. Any property I have belongs to Lady Jane, my legal wife, who unlike you has not been able to present me with a son. The inheritance I'd promised you doesn't exist, I'm afraid. I had intended to write a book about my latest triumph and dedicate the royalties to you and our son. But as I lay here dying, in the icy embrace of the Polar Sea, there is no triumph and there is no book. We must collect our royalties in the Great Beyond, where perhaps I will find the strength to deliver this letter to you and proclaim to all the Blessed the affection I have for you.

Your Loving,
Sir John

The Gripper whistled through a gap between his occasional teeth. The gap was big and the whistle low. "Your Loving Sir John. Well, isn't he the fancy one? Why be fancy if you can't be rich? Seems like the worst of both worlds to me."

Frankie and Donald sifted through the small pile of personal effects, lingering over the medal. Donald looked a little green around the gills, as if he were coming down with something. "Well, I guess it must be the pictures, then, right? Let me take a look over here."

Frankie nodded at the pile of artifacts. "Help yourself then, Donnie."

The tall thief shuffled through the sun pictures. "They don't look like much to me—a few blokes standing next to a British flag. Anybody who would pay big money for this must have more greenies than he knows how to spend. How we doing on time there, Mickey?"

That, I guess, was the Canadian pilot. He'd never been addressed by name before. I'd assumed that he either didn't have a name or the thieves didn't know what it was. He said, "Another ten minutes, maybe fifteen. That's the Adelaide Peninsula down there on the left."

I rubbernecked the nearest window. The peninsula looked like a three-fingered hand clawing at the pack ice collecting off its shore. Landward of the peninsula was the celestial glow of sun on ice. In some places I couldn't tell where the land stopped and the pack ice began. Some fresh snow had fallen to make it all look the same.

"What about the stiff?" the pilot said.

Frankie picked up the things he had found on Sir John's corpse. He put the letters and the sun pictures into a side pocket of his coat. He wrapped the knife and the watch in the tattered handkerchief, and pinned the medal to the lapel of Sir John's naval uniform. Frankie said, "I want to bury him good and proper so's my sister can't find him and he can rest in peace."

The pilot pushed his sunglasses up off the tip of his nose. "He was a sailor, eh? So let's bury him at sea."

Frankie grabbed a Parachute Survive Pak and rolled

Sir John over on his belly. Juice leaked out of the autopsy hole as he struggled to strap on the parachute, a task complicated by the fact that no amount of effort could bend those frozen arms. When this had been accomplished, Frankie pushed his ancestor over to the open hatch and said, "Thanks for the pictures, Gramps."

We waited for a few more minutes, until the Adelaide Peninsula gave way to open sea. Frankie grabbed the rip cord and gave the corpse a shove. The parachute unfolded like a springtime flower blossom. Frankie whispered a Latin prayer as Sir John drifted toward his last resting place. It reminded me of the Catholic Church before they took all the mystery out. The mystery was always my favorite part, not knowing for sure just what the priest was saying and not really understanding what the fuss was all about. The mystery was more believable before they tried to solve it. I wondered if Frankie had been an altar boy too. He knew his Latin well.

"*. . . in nominee Patri, et Feli, et Spiritu Sancti Amen.*"

The pilot flew in a circle for a while, so Frankie could see his ancestor claimed by the Polar Sea. For a moment after he landed, the parachute looked like a lonely ice floe that had become separated from the pack; then it disappeared. Frankie sniffled. Maybe he had a cold coming on. "He always made me feel like I was respectable. The problem with that is, the Irish don't respect respectable. There's something English about being respectable."

The pilot headed south again. Donald said to me, "All right, sport. It's your turn now, only you don't get a parachute."

I explained my position on the matter. There were

laws against this sort of thing, at least in America. Think about all the bad publicity. Consider the consequences. The Gripper considered the consequences, then smiled his gap-toothed, jack-o-lantern smile. I wonder if pumpkins get gingivitis too? He paralyzed me with a kick in the stomach, and used a bungi cord to tie my hands. He was rolling me toward the hatch when Donald said, "Hang on a jiff, will you, Grip? We got some islands coming up ahead. With the way our luck is going, he'll land on one and the Mounties'll find him in the spring."

Frankie shrugged his shoulders and shook his head. The Cessna played a one-note funeral song, the pulsating buzz of engines in harmony. Most of my body was numb. The parts that weren't, my head and my ribs, felt like they were splitting apart. I pictured myself falling into the sea without a parachute, and hoped I'd be dead, or at least unconscious, before I hit the water.

Nobody said much after that, especially me. My life flashed before my eyes. It was not a pretty sight. Mom. Nuns. Where's Dad? The Puerto Ricans down the street. Maria Gutierrez, Rachel Morgan, and too many women in between. Stories I should've written, and other stories I shouldn't have. Mostly I thought about the child I'd never seen, and wondered what would happen to him or her. Would he or she live an untroubled life, or be haunted by the past I'd bequeathed? Where's Dad?

"Okay," Donald said. "Let's do it now."

The Gripper dragged me over to the hatch and started to open it. I kicked at him with my one good foot, so he smacked me on the side of my head. The hatch popped open. I was dizzy and groggy, but a chilling blast of arctic air kept me from passing out. I must have tried to kick him again because he gave me another crack on the head. That's when I slipped into my last dream, the dream that doesn't end. My body didn't hurt anymore. I wasn't even sure I had a body until the Cessna hit a big bump that bounced me against the wall. I came to my senses and used all of them all at once. I remember it all in superslow motion, so things must have happened superfast:

I'm still alive and the Gripper scrambling around on the floor, reaching for a hunting knife that he'd dropped.

Donald cringing by the Parachute Survive Paks and Frankie pointing a gun at him. Frankie shouting, "Gripper! Be still!" but the Gripper keeps going for the knife. Frankie fires and the bullet makes a wet, plopping sound as it buries itself in the flesh of his upper arm. The Gripper stops reaching after that, and becomes very, very still, like a mouse when the cat's about.

"Frankie," Donald said. "What're you doing here? This is the second time in a row that you're trying to cheat the gang. Ned Kelly will be very disappointed. They'll be coming after you."

But Frankie didn't want to talk to Donald. He talked to the pilot instead. "Here's the way it is, sport. It's time for you to get on the winning team."

The pilot looked at Frankie's gun. Then he looked at his instruments. "I'm right here, eh? What kind of deal you talking about?"

Frankie kept the gun moving. Sometimes he pointed it at Donald and sometimes at the Gripper. He said, "You get Donnie's ten percent and I get all the rest. Your paycheck'll be a couple of hundred thousand pounds if what they say is true. That's a lot of Canadian dollars, right? You can buy yourself a brand-new plane. One that doesn't have blood all over."

"What about your pals?" the pilot said.

"The way I see it is we throw them all out. We'll go faster and farther with a lighter load."

"I don't want to kill anybody unless it is necessary. You're going back to Australia, but I've got to live around here."

Frankie thought about it, then said, "Of course, everybody gets a parachute, and we'll drop them out over solid land. We can even call the Mounties when we stop to refuel so they can send out a rescue party. I'm not a killer at heart. Everybody gets a fighting chance, even the Radio Star. He's just along for the ride anyway."

They dropped us over the northern shore of mainland Canada.

Free-fall was like a nightmare, a bitter cold rush at death. After the chute popped open, it was more like a very weird dream. The prevailing wind was a bone-chilling blast from the south that pushed me back out over the pack ice and toward the open sea. To my right I could see the soft pillow-tops of Donald's and Frankie's chutes. To my left I saw the Cessna disappear into the southern sky.

Below me was the pack ice shifting on the polar sea. It looked like the surface of the moon might look if the moon was made of frosted glass.

I saw that Donald and the Gripper were drifting toward shore while I was dropping straight down toward the open sea. Then I remembered one of those stray facts that hang around in the rarely used parts of our brains, hoping they'll be used someday. I'd read someplace, sometime, that a parachute could be guided by tugging on its strings. I tugged on the strings closest to the mainland, but that set me off in the wrong direction. Next I tugged on the strings opposite that point, and that seemed to do the trick. While it didn't propel me back to land, it did stop what was certainly a fatal seaward drift. As I got close to touching down, I could hear a low, steady grinding sound as the pack made more ice from the choppy sea and squeezed it against the beach.

I bounced against the slippery side of an iceberg that was trapped by the annual winter freeze. The parachute crumpled, but a snowdrift helped to break my fall, and I landed with only a bruise or two.

It felt like I landed on a very large water bed. I didn't sink, but neither did I feel that the pack ice was very stable. I climbed out from under the parachute membrane that billowed around me and quickly examined the contents of the Survive Pak. It contained: a warm down parka with an adjustable hood, a small but businesslike handgun with a box of bullets, six cans of sterno, a compass, several maps, two chocolate bars, six cans of Certified Protein Product —property of the Alaska National Guard, a knife, some rope, a flashlight, three flares, sixty-four ounces of Certified Multi-Nutrition Food Substance, some matches, three gallons of Blasto, and a small pamphlet with instructions on how to use these things. The parachute doubled as a tent.

I put on the parka and adjusted the hood, then started walking toward the mainland. Every now and then, I checked the compass to make sure I was headed south.

Sometimes, the surface of the pack ice produced a subtle yet pervasive vibration, like a fancy car in its lowest gear. If I stood very still and looked very hard, it seemed that the mainland was moving. Of course, that was an illusion. I was the one that was moving, along with the shifting ice. But no matter how hard I looked, I couldn't tell in which direction it was shifting—north, south, east, west, or something in between. If the pack ice was moving toward the beach, the distance got shorter the longer I waited. If not, the ice might crack open right under my feet. Maybe I'd bob about in the water for a while, until the heat was drained from my body in a natural and orderly way. First the fingers and the toes; then the arms and legs. The heart and brain would shut down last. Perhaps I would have some demented vision caused by the chill on my brain.

I tied the rope to the hunting knife and used this contraption as a climbing tool to get over the smooth mounds of ice that rippled over the pack like waves of a storm frozen in place. I climbed all day but didn't get far. I took a number of detours around holes and cracks in the ice, and around slippery ice barriers that were impossible to surmount. I spent at least two hours climbing out of a crevasse created by two icebergs that had been fused together by the freeze.

In order to escape this trap, I had to hack sturdy handholds every foot or so, then pray that I would be able to haul the Survive Pak up after me. This took another half hour or so, as the bundle was very heavy and the ice was very slick.

The ice turned gray and the sky turned black, so I flipped my cheap sunglasses into the up position and looked for a solid place to camp. A hundred thousand billion stars filled the northern night, but I did not pause to wonder at their beauty. I was too busy reading detailed instructions by flashlight:

Step 1: Your parachute can be made into a water-proof tent. It is designed to conserve heat to the maximum possible degree. The heat value of the Blasto Petroleum Jelly will be wasted if it is ignited before the parachute/tent is pitched. (See Step 24.)

It took me a while to get to Step 24. The wind howled like a hound from hell while the temperature dropped into a bottomless pit. The cold made my hands numb and clumsy, complicating the task of attaching Hook #5 to Ring #3. When the tent was filled with Blasto heat and my feet were starting to thaw, I had a bite to eat. The Certified Protein Product tasted like soybeans and chewed like peanut butter. The Certified Multi-Nutritional Food Substance didn't taste like anything. It was a computer's idea of what food should be.

"Screw it," I said to myself as I reached for one of the chocolate bars. I stuffed the other one in the pocket of my parka and forgot about it for a while.

I woke up before the sun came up so I wouldn't waste any time. I packed up the tent and ate some Certified Protein Product. My watch said it was 8:38 A.M. back on the Bodenburg Butte, but there was still no sign of the sun. The nights were now longer than the days, and I was starting to think that I'd probably die if I didn't make mainland pretty soon. If one must die, and I guess one must, he should do it in the arctic, where death is its own anesthetic and even corpses have a purpose in life, to provide riches to undeserving surfers and meat to deserving dogs.

The eastern sky started to glow. I flipped my cheap sunglasses down. It looked like another clear day. I saw blue sky and white snow, towering icebergs, and the shadow of a man standing off to my left with his back to the rising sun.

"Oh, shit!" I said. I was starting to talk to myself. I couldn't tell who the shadow was, but I knew it was looking at me. I hoisted the Parachute Survive Pak onto my shoulders and started to walk toward the shadow, which was about a hundred yards away.

The shadow started walking too. It kept its distance from me. When I stopped, it stopped. When I walked fast, it walked faster. It was almost as if the shadow were my own dark image superimposed on a distant silver screen. It never let me get too close or too far. One time I hid behind an iceberg to see what it would do. It waited for me like a patient parent. Another time I veered right at an angle that would take me toward the mainland but away from its disturbing presence. The shadow changed direction too and the distance between us remained the same.

It stopped being a shadow shortly after noon, when the sun started to shed some light on the side that was closest to me. It was the Gripper, and he had a Survive Pak too. I noticed that he carried his with a lot less strain.

"What's the game?" I screamed at him.

At first I thought he hadn't heard me. But after a while, he screamed back: "Just want to keep an eye on you. Make sure that you're okay."

When I stopped to eat some Certified Protein Product, he stopped to eat something too. This might have gone on for quite some time if I hadn't fallen into another crevasse.

I didn't even see it coming. I had one eye on the Gripper and the other on the mainland. One minute I was crawling through a snowdrift and the next minute both the drift and I were on a very fast downward plunge. It felt like a water-slide, only steeper and deeper and very much more unstable. There was that grinding sound again, only much louder now, and it seemed to me that the sides of the crevasse were either collapsing together or splitting apart.

I was in trouble in any case. I tried to climb out but couldn't. The walls were too steep for that.

The Gripper must have waited for an hour or so before he came and took a look. During that time I decided that the crevasse was splitting apart. A pool of water was starting to form about ten feet from the ice-niche that I had carved for myself with the blade of my National Guard hunting knife. The pool was becoming a flood that would have inundated me had the Gripper not come to my assistance for reasons of his own.

He seemed pleased that I was uninjured, and unimpressed by the gun I was pointing in his direction. He had a bloody spot on his upper arm, where Frankie's bullet had pierced his flesh.

He said, "So you got a gun too, right. It's hard to kill a man. I know because I've done it. You ever use a gun before?"

I attempted a pitiful snarl which was worse than saying no.

"Here's the way I see it, sport. You got a gun and so do I, only you're stuck and I'm not. If I let you out then we'll both have guns and maybe you'll take a shot at me. I don't want to die is all. So give me your gun and I'll help you out. Otherwise I'm on my way."

"Why?"

"Why what, mate?"

"Why do you want to help me? I'll only slow you down."

He picked his words carefully. "I'm a sociable person, and I don't want to die. I save your life and you save mine."

"How?"

"How what, mate?"

"How am I going to save your life?"

"We can talk about that some other time. You'll be too wet to save if I don't get you out in a jiff. Water kills when it's cold like this. Now be a sport and give me the gun."

We walked together for a while. The Gripper was very concerned about me, and slowed his pace to accommodate mine. He even offered to carry part of my load. "I can carry the food if you want, since you've got that gimpy leg."

"That's okay. I'm doing fine. So whatever happened to Donnie? I thought that you two landed together."

He didn't answer me.

The pack ice became more solid the closer we got to the mainland. But sometimes it felt like we were riding a very slow wave with a very big surfboard. In one of these places, the Gripper grabbed my elbow and whispered, "Stop. Be quiet. Don't make a sound."

I didn't make a sound and neither did he. I even stopped breathing for a while, until my lungs felt like they were caving in. The ice we were standing on rolled and rocked while we listened to the noises of the north: grinding ice, howling wind, and the sound of something heavy slapping something wet.

I sipped some air and used it to whisper. "Sounds like some kind of animal. A seal or a walrus, maybe."

"Or maybe a polar bear. You heard what that Eskimo fellow said. There's lots of bears around here."

We backed away and took another detour. The ice stopped shifting, and the slapping diminished until we couldn't hear it anymore. By the time we got back on track and were again walking in the general direction of the mainland, the southern sky was turning gray and night was on the march. I flipped up my cheap sunglasses.

We walked until the sun went down, but the island still seemed far away. This lent credence to my theory that the pack was drifting away from the island at about the same speed that we were walking toward it. I said, "It's like we're walking up the down escalator. I bet we could walk for a week and never move an inch."

"Shut up, okay?" the Gripper said.

I shut up for a while but couldn't control myself. "So whatever happened to Donald? Maybe he found a way out of here."

"Shut up, okay?" the Gripper said.

We pitched our tents in a large ice cave formed by the juncture of two icebergs. After that, it was time to eat. That's when the Gripper said, "Hey, Pres?"

The way he said it made me think that his greatest ambition in life was to be my closest friend. "Hey what?" I said.

"How much food have you got left?"

Friends to the end. I tried to think of five things at once, which was at least four too many. If I lie, then X. If I don't, then Y. He's got the guns and he's faster than me. If I told him a little lie, I might get away with it.

"Not much," I said. "I ate the chocolate bars first. How about you?"

"That's the problem, mate. I don't have any food. They must have pulled a boner when they packed my pack. When I asked Donald to give me some food he ran away from me. How's that for being my chum? I was hoping maybe you'd give me some of your food, remembering how I saved your life."

I think he was lying about the food, but that didn't matter. He didn't exactly point a gun at me, but he did point his chin at the gun he carried in the pocket of his coat. He kept the other gun hidden in his boot, I think.

"Sure, Grip, why not?"

I offered him a cup of Protein Product. He thanked me a lot and took three instead. When he was done he said, "Are you sure you ate both of those chocolate bars? Some sweets would be a bonzer treat."

"Bonzer?"

"You know, 'crash hot.' You Yanks say 'groovy,' I guess."

I told him I'd already eaten both of the chocolate bars. After much consideration, he decided to believe me. We crawled into our parachute-tents. He slept. I didn't.

In the morning he told me he'd had a dream.

"It's the strangest dream I've ever had. I was a man named Torrington and I'd signed up as a sailor on one of those ships that Sir Johnny Franklin had. The *Terror,* I think it was. We were very hungry because the food ran out. And what happened is Johnny had his heart attack, so they called us all over to the other ship—the *Erebus,* I think it was. It was a grand old ship—three hundred and seventy tons and a hundred and five feet long. It had everything but food. We all crowded into his cabin. It was dark and it smelled like part of him had died already. He wanted to give us some good-bye advice, since he knew he was going to croak."

He stopped talking here, so I could ask questions. I didn't ask any questions because I didn't want to know the answers.

"So we all huddled in close to hear what he had to say, and he said the craziest thing."

Again he paused and again I didn't say anything. "Do you know what he said?"

"No, I don't."

"He said, 'Eat me, boys. It's only meat.' What do you think he meant by that?"

He had this obsessive need to talk about it, as if confessing his crime in advance would make it less of a sin.

"I could never eat people pie," he said. He was chewing on some of my food at the time. It was high noon of the third day and the mainland was finally in striking distance. With luck we would camp on the beach that night.

"I could never eat people pie," he repeated, in case I hadn't heard him. "But there's some that can, you know. When I was a kid back home in Oz they used to tell this story about an Irishman called Alexander Pearce. You're Irish, right? Could you ever eat people pie?"

I told him that I couldn't, wouldn't, and shouldn't; that the very idea was so disgusting that I didn't even want to talk about it.

"They say it tastes like pork, you know."

He took another one of those long pauses. This time, I couldn't stand it. "And who's they?" I said.

"They would be Alexander Pearce, the one I'm trying to tell you about."

"And who's Alexander Pearce?"

He was a national legend with a taste for crime,

literature, and human flesh. The Gripper told me all about him.

"Here's the what's what as far as them stories go. Alexander was an Irishman who stole six pairs of shoes one time and got sentenced to life in Oz. He almost escaped across the desert two different times, and both times he did it by eating his mates. First time there were seven men with him and he made it all the way to Jericho before he got caught by the Regimentals. The blues was quite impressed because no bolter ever got that far neither before or never since. For some crazy reason, Alexander confessed his crime, but the blues didn't believe him. They thought he was covering up so's the mates he'd ate could get away. They flogged him a good one and sent him back to the penny at Macquarie Harbor. Of course, the old crawlers all had to know just how he did it, but Alexander wouldn't say. This one fellow begged him to tell so's he could try it too. So Alexander Pearce says, 'Hey, mate, I don't have to tell you. Come along with me and I'll show you how it's done.' Well, the second time he didn't get too far, and this time they caught him with some leftovers in his pocket. Alexander, being an Irishman, wrote a book about it. It was a short book because they hanged him right away. You can't have some crazy Irishman eating people pie. Prester John Riordan's an Irish name, right?"

We walked in silence for a while, each in our own little world. My world was fully of jolly carnivores. A polar bear played cards with the Gripper for the right to gobble me down while some brilliant Irish scribbler took notes for a book he intended to write. What about the Gripper's little world? What was that place like? He left it for a moment so that he could talk to me:

"Here's what I don't understand. See, what Alexander Pearce did was kill his mates first and then chew them down. What I would do if I was him is keep them alive as long as I could. Starting with finger sandwiches and then maybe eating a handburger."

He said this with a straight face. Puns were not intended.

"I'd work my way to the arms and then up to the shoulders. See that way my mate could still walk along like cattle on the hoof. The meat'd stay fresher that way and I wouldn't have to carry it."

I can still see the big black headline that kept rolling off the presses of an imaginary tabloid newspaper: I WAS EATEN ALIVE BY A MAN WITH ADVANCED GINGIVITIS! (Pictures and story inside.)

We walked in silence until we reached the northern beach of mainland Canada. The last few yards of pack ice were crammed so tightly against the shore that it rolled up into great ice mountains that were hard to climb and obstructed our view. We lost sight of our destination just as we were about to reach it.

"Quiet! What's that?" the Gripper said.

At first I didn't hear anything. The older I get, the deafer I become. This is a sore point with Rachel, who thinks that I can only hear the things I want to hear. After a while, however, if I kept very still and held my breath, I could hear the soft but steady drone of an engine in the distance.

I hoisted the Parachute Survive Pak off my shoulders and retrieved the three flares that it contained. The instructions seemed simple enough: Tear off the top and rub it against the bottom to ignite the stuff that flashes and smokes. I was going to do just that when the Gripper said, "Now take it easy, mate. You better let me do that."

The droning buzz was louder. The plane was coming our way. I pretended that Gripper hadn't said anything and lighted the flare anyway. He was on me right away, crushing the hand that held the flare with his own iron fist. The flare dropped onto the ice. He jammed it into a snowbank, hot end first. This made a sizzling sound as the red flash was extinguished. The small cloud of smoke it had produced drifted over the pack ice like a patch of polluted fog.

"What're you trying to do?" I said. "Frankie said he'd call the Mounties. That plane is trying to rescue us."

"Rescue you and arrest me. That's the way I see it. Maybe it's a Mountie plane, or maybe it's those scientists. Either way it's bad news for the Gripper. I hope you wouldn't want anything bad to happen to me."

We waited for the plane to show itself. It was a Mountie plane, painted a bright, redcoat red. I wondered if it had an emblem on the side: We always get our man—whether he did it or not. It flew right overhead, but didn't see us down below. The Gripper held me down so I couldn't wave my arms. I screamed as loudly as I could, but the engine noise must have obliterated any sound I made.

The Gripper let me go when the plane was out of sight. He said, "I worry about you Irish sometimes. If you're not telling stories to the blues, then you're eating people pie. I better keep an eye on you."

I didn't think fast, but I did think clearly. As we climbed down from the icy sea onto the snow-covered beach, the first few buds of a notion started to sprout in my brain. It wasn't a full-fledged plan. That would have had to include a physical triumph over the

Gripper, transportation back to Alaska, and a story in either the *National Enquirer* or the *New York Times,* whichever paid the fastest and the most. I didn't have a plan to achieve these things, but I did have the first few buds of a notion. Perhaps I could spoil the Gripper's appetite.

"Hey Gripper," I said. "I'm not feeling very good."

We had just pitched our tents and eaten the last of the Certified Protein Product. There was half a can of the other stuff left.

"What's wrong?" He sounded very concerned, and in a way I guess he was.

"I think it's the hypothermia starting to kick in. You've heard of hypothermia, right?"

Now it was my turn to pause and his turn to think things over. "I can't say as I have, mate. Why don't you tell me about it."

That was back in 1986. This was after I'd met Rachel but before I'd declared my affection. I'd been riding around in a snow machine on the frozen surface of the Toyukuk River. Things went wrong and I got lost. A storm came and the temperature dropped. I suffered a bout of hypothermia and felt the hard nip of frostbite in the toes of my polio foot.

"I started to get a gangrene fever so they chopped off two of my toes," I said.

The Gripper was very interested. He'd heard of gangrene before.

I showed him my polio foot. It wasn't a pretty sight. Shiny scars marked the surgeon's work, and the toes I did have were skinny and bent out of shape. He thought about things for a while. "Gangrene's not contagious, right? You got it from freezing your foot."

I said, "No, gangrene's not contagious. But polio is another story. That's what's wrong with my leg, you know. I had a run-in with polio. Polio, gangrene, hypothermia. I've been through a lot. Anybody makes a pie out of me better have a pretty strong stomach."

He thought about this, or about something else. I'm pretty sure he was thinking, because his forehead became wrinkled up, and he stared off into space, looking at things he could not see.

CHAPTER 23

By morning the Gripper had decided that he really didn't want to be my friend. Polio, gangrene, and hypothermia may have saved me from a grisly, if exotic, fate, but this didn't improve my situation. Now he wanted to steal my food.

"Hand it over, mate. That and all your Blasto. I'm making a run for it, and I'm not waiting around for you. What I'll do is see if Donald's around, or maybe if he found some way to get out of here. If that's how it is, then I'll be gone. If that's how it isn't, then I'll be back. So you take care of yourself, okay?"

As he stomped off, heading west along the coast, I watched the brightening glow of dawn and wished I had something to eat. Then I remembered the chocolate bar. I ate half and saved half for later.

This day was shorter and colder than the one before, and a polar wind kicked up some trouble. I followed the trail the Gripper had made in the snow along the beach. The beach felt like a cold chisel pounding on a slab of corrugated steel that had been kept in a freezer on the dark side of the moon, the side that hasn't seen the sun in more than a billion years. I felt about a hundred different kinds of cold. I can only list a few: the ripping, slicing cold of the wind, the constant, forever cold of the permafrost beneath my feet, the sloppy cold of the snow, and the cold that kills but doesn't hurt at all—the numb, clumpy cold of frostbite nipping on the toe tips of my polio foot. I felt hot but didn't sweat; or maybe that was the start of a gangrene dream.

Later on—how much later, I can't really say—I thought I heard something. Maybe it was the promise of possibility and hope, or maybe it was part of a gangrene dream. It sounded like the barking of a dog. The more I walked the louder it became. My polio foot didn't feel a thing.

I remember the cold, the wind, and the gut pile, and other things that may or may not have happened. But mostly I remember the dog, and the thin thread of hope that his barking inspired in me. I talked to myself some more and started calling him Eugene. That's the name that my mother gave to the first dog I ever had. The old Eugene was part poodle and part everything else. Every now and then my mother would get him a French poodle cut: hair cropped close on the body and limbs, with a black puff at the tip of his tail. Eugene was friendly to me and other children but hostile to my mother and other adults, probably because they named him Eugene and gave him silly haircuts. We were the best of friends and had a grand old time until he bit a meter reader who deserved it, in my opinion. My mother had Eugene destroyed for that. The last thing I remember is the way he looked at me. His tail drooped between his legs. He knew he'd been betrayed but he loved me anyway. That's the thing about dogs. They love you anyway.

I was so intent on the barking and my memories of Eugene, that I didn't even realize I'd walked into a gut pile; that of a walrus, I presume. Protruding from the bloody gore of hair, meat, and bones were two enormous teeth. They were each about a foot long and shaped like cribbage pegs. I sorted through these leftovers and tried not to think about how many animals had done this already: first the polar bear, then the scavengers—dogs, birds, lemmings, and the Gripper. One dead walrus could feed a lot of animals, but there wasn't much left for me: five chunks of chewy gristle, the stuff that holds the bones together. I gnawed on what looked like a piece of walrus nose. It was covered with blood and frozen to a delicate crunch. I washed it down with melted snow, then continued on my way, my boots soaked with blubber and blood.

The meal revived my spirits and gave me some energy. I needed energy desperately because I couldn't stop walking anymore. Even with a proper tent, I'd freeze for sure without Blasto. Even if I did wake up, my polio foot would never thaw. I'd have another bout with hypothermia and a real case of gangrene, not just a disgusting story to spoil the Gripper's appetite. Real gangrene was a nightmare of pain and fever, or so I'd been told by the man who'd saved my life by chopping off my toes.

His name was Reggie Moore and he was the mayor of Toyukuk City. When I woke up he said to me, "I seen gangrene when I did my duty in Burma. The skin starts to rot away and it raises a horrible stink."

I tried not to think about Reggie or gangrene. I listened to the dog. What was he barking at?

I couldn't stop for the night. That would be the death of me. I flipped up my cheap sunglasses and walked as fast as I could walk on a foot that couldn't feel anything.

The sky over the ice pack throbbed with brilliant colors as the wispy shades of the northern lights shifted from green to gold to red and back to green again, like Kodachrome ghosts that have lost their way. It would be so nice to lie down on the beach and watch the northern lights, and then take that nap that would never end. How painless could it get?

I kept on walking toward the dog. Feed a dog once a day and he's your friend for life. The dog sounded very close now. So close that I could even hear what he was howling at. There was a two-part animal harmony.

Sometimes the dog would howl, or wimper, or even keep quiet for a moment. But the *grrrr* was always there, a throaty doo-wop that never stopped. I stood still for a moment. It seemed that the *howoooo* was on my right and the *grrrr* was on my left. I veered right, toward the pack ice crunching against the beach.

I must have heard wrong, because after I'd taken a step or two, the *grrrrr* stopped altogether. The dog stopped howling and the wind died down. I didn't move a muscle. The pounding of my heart sounded like a timpani. I stood still for a very long time, until shapes started to emerge in the orange light of dawn. I moved to flip down my cheap sunglasses, but I'd lost them during the night. Dawn bathed the snow with a light so bright it burned my eyes.

* * *

Sea fog seeped up through cracks in the ice and glittered as it turned to frost. The *grrrrr* had been produced by two polar bears frolicking on the pack ice, a large mama and her troublesome baby. The cub ran circles around its mother and performed a series of astonishing somersaults, which the mama attempted to ignore. She stopped pacing as soon as I made a move and watched me with intent curiosity. The cub seemed to resent the fact that her attention was directed elsewhere, and climbed onto its mama's lap and started pawing at her belly. Maybe the cub scratched too hard or maybe the mother was suspicious of me. In either case, the big bear stood up on its hind legs and uttered a terrible cry. The cub tumbled to the ice and performed another somersault. It looked to its mother for approval, but Mama Bear was still growling at me.

The polar bear dog was tied to a stake a few hundred yards up the beach. It also had some company. The Gripper was standing by, just beyond the reach of the chain to which the dog was tied. The thief greeted me as I abandoned the position I had held for most of the night. "I figured it was you," he said. "I knew you'd be along. There's nobody else out here, sport. Donnie's disappeared someplace, and I still ain't seen any sign of whoever owns this dog. Have you been eating regular?"

I turned toward the dog, so that I could ignore the question. Through the blinding glare of this bright, white hell, I could see that it was more like a wolf than a dog and didn't look at all like the old Eugene. He was a tough, scrawny beast with long legs, sharply pointed ears, and a heavily muscled jaw. He wasn't barking at the polar bears. He was barking at the Gripper, who said, "I was hoping that the owner would come along and show us a way to get out of here. I'm about ready to give up on that pretty soon."

The polar bears stopped growling for a moment while they sniffed the air and licked their chops. The dog barked louder and strained harder against his chain. Mama bear dropped down on all fours and the dog stopped barking for a moment. The Gripper fired a shot over her head. She snatched the cub to her bosom and gave it a little hug. The Gripper fired another shot and the two bears dropped out of sight.

My ears tingled and my scalp started to sweat. "Where'd they go?" I said.

"Don't know and don't care. I guess I must have showed them the what's what, right? That's what they get for making noise at me."

I studied the pack ice, but it all looked the same to me. Bright blue sky and light blue ice punctuated by icebergs and ice floes frozen into place by onset of winter. It was unstained and unblemished. Even the dirt looked clean. I thought I saw an ice floe move, but it must have been my imagination. Nothing would move until spring came and the thaw gave the icebergs leave to continue their journey south.

"That's a good boy," the Gripper said, loading some bullets into his gun. His eyes were nervous and his smile was forced, which was how he'd looked when he told me the story of Alexander Pearce.

The dog stopped barking and started to cry. "Easy, boy. Easy," the Gripper said. "Just sit still for a second and it'll be over before you know it."

"Wait," I said. "What are you doing?"

"I'm fixing my dinner, arsehole. And you're not getting any."

Before he could pull the trigger I said, "You're making a big mistake."

He turned around and pointed the gun at me. His hands were shaking and his teeth were clenched. He was crazy, just like the pilot said. "How's that, sport?"

I had lots of reasons, and listed them as quickly as my fevered brain could think them: The hybrid hadn't done him any harm and didn't have much meat on his bones; he'd saved our lives by guiding us to this place; perhaps he could save our lives again by guiding us to the home of his master; he'd been keeping the polar bears at bay.

None of this made any sense to the Gripper, who'd already made up his mind. "The polar bears're gone, sport, and my stomach's talking to me. They say Chinks eat dogs, you know, and Chinks're very smart people. Very healthy too. Chinks never get cancer."

The dog rolled over and peed all over itself, which is what wolves do when submitting themselves to the will of man or other wolves. Then the Gripper blew a hole in its head. A pathetic wimper gurgled in his throat as his life spilled onto the snow. Dog is man's best friend, but man does not reciprocate.

"That was a mistake," I said.

"Buzz off, arsehole. I'd be doing you if I hadn't done him. It's your turn next if we don't get out of here real soon."

He rummaged through his Parachute Survive Pak for the hunting knife with the serrated edge. I turned my eyes away as he prepared to apply it to his prey. I thought I saw an ice floe move. It must have been my imagination, or maybe it was the pack ice shifting on the frozen sea, or the specter of a gangrene dream, or the drifting of snow upon the wind, or two hungry polar bears sneaking up on us. I sat down, watched the pack ice, and waited for something to happen.

The Eskimos were right to feed their flesh to the

dogs. What better way to reward man's best friend? Feed me to the dogs when I die. Or feed me to the polar bears. Or feed me to the fishes or the rats or the worms or the vultures or the lemmings or the cockroaches. Just don't feed me to the Gripper. He eats like an animal and chews with his mouth half open.

My belly was empty, my foot was numb, and my brain was catching a fever. My eyes teared up as the hot glare of sun on snow burned them to a boil. Maybe I really did have gangrene. Maybe the Gripper would eat me and die. That would be a revenge of sorts. No more angry days and no more lonely nights. No more Rachel. No more news. Just the big black hole of sweet oblivion. Nothing is better than something when you had it all and threw it away. My life had been full of regrets about all those might-have-beens. My death might be more of the same, but maybe it wouldn't hurt so much.

"Listen, sport," the Gripper said. "I think you got the wrong idea."

I didn't have any ideas. Ideas are nothing but trouble. "How's that?" I think I said. I'm not sure of anything anymore.

He was going to explain, but never got the chance. His jaw went slack and his eyes popped open. A half-chewed piece of dog meat fell out of his mouth and onto his lap. He jumped to his feet and pointed his gun at something I couldn't see. I shaded my eyes as good as I could. The snow was getting a pinkish hue. I said, "I told you you shouldn't have killed the dog. He was keeping the bears at bay."

"Shut up, you goddamn Potato Peeler. Can't you see there's a bear out there? What're we going to do?"

I thought about that for a moment. "I think we're going to die."

Mama Bear was bigger than a small Japanese automobile. Her fur was white with a tinge of yellow. Her eyes were pink and her mouth was purple. She reared up on her hind legs and scratched the sky with her claws.

I closed my eyes and thought about Rachel. I hoped she would find a decent man, raise our child straight and strong, and think about me every now and then with something besides disgust. I opened my eyes for a moment. The cub watched with interest while Mama Bear walked in a circle. The Gripper walked in a circle too. I was in the middle. I closed my eyes again and thought about our child. I wondered if it was a he or a she and choked on the sad fact that I would never know. I hoped my child would live a good life and think about me every now and then with something besides disgust. When I opened my eyes I saw that the Gripper had stopped in his tracks and Mama Bear was looking at me.

A brave person is often a person who doesn't have any other choice. I kept very still and didn't scream as Mama Bear dropped down on all fours and poked her nose at my polio foot, the one with all the maladies. She sniffed once and almost gagged.

The Gripper made a blubbering sound and started to back away; Mama Bear came after him. He fired five sure shots that made five red spots on her fur but didn't slow her charge. He turned on his heels and ran. He took ten steps and she took two. His scream became a gurgle as she ripped his throat open with a short stroke of her left paw, like a mama human taking knife to sausage. The thief's stout heart beat out two great squirts of blood. The rest came out like red wine from a spilled bottle.

Baby Bear trotted up to me. Looked at my throat

and did a somersault. Looked and sniffed at my polio foot. Cleaned its nose with a sneeze. Did another somersault. It might have been cute if I wasn't so scared.

They were very neat in their way, picking the bones clean as could be and licking the bloody snow for dessert. I managed to slip behind a pingo while they were feasting. There was no sense running away as I had no place to run. All I had was a frozen foot, a slender hope, and half of a chocolate bar I'd hidden away. I wolfed it down in three big bites. It tasted a little stale.

CHAPTER 24

Maybe it was the salt sea fog, drenching my clothes and freezing my brain. Maybe it was a whiteout kicked up by a northerly wind. Maybe it was the Eternal Light shining through Death's Door. In any event, I couldn't see a thing unless it was happening inside my head.

My eyes teared and the tears boiled. I thought it was gangrene fever. It's a good thing it wasn't or I'd be dead.

I couldn't see but I could still feel my way through some simple tasks. I used the hunting knife to dig a cave in the ice, lined the cave with the parachute, and then wrapped the ends of the chute around me. I took off my leg brace so that I could wrap my good leg around my frozen foot. That's one thing about a polio leg. It's very flexible. The toes I didn't have started to itch and the ones I did have became hot and tender.

I had a weird, epic dream about the Speaker of the House and Danger Dan Wood, about Sir John Franklin and Maggie Stubbs, about Frankie and his sister, about Rachel and the baby, about people who'd died before I was born, and people who hadn't been born yet. I thought I would dream forever about almost everything, but then I dreamed about a man named Jimmer who wanted to know why his dog was dead. I couldn't see Jimmer's face, but I could hear what he said to me: "You crazy to kill my dog, goddamnit. My dog barks when the polar bears come. You white people are very foolish, so the polar bears came and killed your friend. How come they didn't kill you? Are you okay, eh? I'm talking to you."

They rushed me to the Fort Resolution Territorial Medical Center on the shores of the Great Slave Lake. They put a damp towel over my eyes and kept me in a very dark room. The dark was like a cool drink of water for my parched eyes, and after a few days I could see the first few glimmers and sparks of sight.

The doctor's name was Benjamin Tooliksik. He said I was going to be okay.

"You must have taken your sunglasses off and lost them along the way. That'll make you blind real quick up here, for a little while anyway. Do you remember seeing 'red' for a while?"

I remembered the polar bears, and the way the ice turned pink. I thought it was partly the Gripper's blood and partly gangrene fever.

"That's the first symptom—seeing red. Then you can't see anything. I don't think there's any permanent damage, but there's no way to say for sure. We'll just have to see what you can see."

I knew I was supposed to laugh, but I just didn't have the heart. "What about my foot? Is my foot okay?"

"Your foot is fine, as far as it goes. Except for the polio, of course. I think you had a mild case of food poisoning. That would explain the fever and delirium. What have you been eating?"

I told him I'd been eating army food, chocolate bars, and lots and lots of nothing. "Maybe it was that walrus nose. I ate a walrus nose, I think. Or it could have been a walrus ear."

"I don't think it was the walrus. Meat never spoils in the Northwest Territories. It's too damn cold up here. My guess is it was that army food, maybe the chocolate bar. It couldn't have been the Protein Product, or your Mr. Gripper friend would have gotten sick too. What you need now is a little rest and lots of water to flush your system out."

I flushed my system for three whole days and my eyes repaired themselves. When I was fit to travel, I was taken to the Franklin District Headquarters of the Royal Canadian Mounted Police by an Eskimo Mountie with a smooth, chubby face and oriental eyes. We walked along the shores of the Great Slave Lake. The water was still free of ice, but that wouldn't last for long. I felt a familiar chill in the air.

The Mountie sat me in an uncomfortable chair in a room without windows, carpeting, or any other adornment. One of his colleagues, a sturdy man with a broken nose, conducted a formal inquiry. He didn't learn a lot. I described the sun pictures and told him how many millions the photogrammarian thought they were worth. Then I recounted Sir John's burial, the Gripper's demise, and Donald's disappearance.

I said, "They gave the body a parachute too, and dropped it into Queen Maud's Gulf. Like a burial at sea by his own flesh and blood. I'm sure that Sir John would have approved. He was a sailor, you know."

It was hard to tell if he knew or not, but he thought about it for a moment and wrote something down in a Mountie notebook with the Mountie motto and an emblem on its cover. He pursued a new line of inquiry. "Now about this Donald Montague fellow. Where do you think he went?"

I shrugged my shoulders and said I didn't know. The Mountie jotted down a note. He asked some questions more than once, hoping I'd improve on my earlier replies.

"You say this pilot was Canadian, eh?"

Or, "And then they tossed you out of the plane?"

Or, "Now you say that this Gripper fellow was going to eat you alive. How do you know that? What did he say?"

I gave him the disgusting details. He seemed very interested. When I was done he said, "Thank you, Mr. Riordan. That'll be all for now."

CHAPTER 25

Silent snow fell on the Bodenburg Butte. It put a shiver in my bones, as if the flakes were falling on my naked skin. I sat at the station for hours on end, listening to the automated KREL Kountry hits and staring at the telephone. I didn't know what to say, and I didn't know how to say it. I felt like one of those doomed moose, plodding through the underbrush in an endless search for browse that didn't exist anymore.

I had lunch with Dr. Bud. He was the only person I knew who was more depressed than I by the numerous scandals that persisted in the aftermath of the expedition. "Science Today" pulled the plug after Sir John and his sun pictures disappeared from the scene. The producer decided that this was not a proper subject for American public TV. Bandwagons travel in reverse sometimes. The Petco Petroleum Company complained about the wasted use of their Vibroseise Device and the Alaska National Guard reported the theft of several Parachute Survive Paks. The Speaker's Republican enemies sniffed the scent of political blood. They denounced Gertevorst for urging the National Guard to commit the Hercules C-130 to such a debacle.

All of this was dully recorded in the *Matanuska News-Nugget,* including a bitchy commentary written by Stephanie Kirsten. They talked about it at Peg's Pharmacy and they talked about it on "Trapline." They talked about it wherever people talk, which in Palmer is just about everyplace. Danger Dan posted a sign about it on the back of his gravel truck. The Speaker was forced to defend himself on the floor of the House.

He said, "I do not understand why the scientific use of a single military plane should provoke such bitter comment from my distinguished colleagues in the House. Thousands of military planes have attempted millions of military missions over the years, but I'll wager that none of them was engaged in an enterprise as noble as the Hercules C-130 of the Alaska National Guard that is now in question here. This plane wasn't delivering weapons of death to some unfortunate Third World country. And it wasn't delivering brave soldiers to a hostile situation. It was delivering scientists to a cold and forsaken place so they could do battle with ignorance, the most dangerous enemy of all. It is unfortunate that our Australian guests did not achieve all of their objectives, but that's no reason to condemn their heroic attempt."

Dr. Bud was not consoled by this, and he wasn't consoled by a breaded veal cutlet and a piece of Peg's Pie that I treated him to one day. He chewed without enjoyment and paused for an artificial sigh, as might be heard at a funeral for somebody with few friends but many acquaintances.

"That's it," he said. "There's nothing else for me. No virus-free seed potato and no appearance on 'Science Today.' Do you know what really gets me?"

I shook my head. Bud tried to spear a piece of pie crust, but only managed to break it into crumbs too small to eat. He surrendered his fork to the plate, and used a wet tip of his finger to blot up a few morsels. Peg poured us a fresh round of coffee and asked him if he wanted another piece of pie. Bud nodded reluctantly. He was taking refuge in food even though he couldn't taste it anymore.

"What really gets me is they had the Palmer High School band back over at the airport to greet us when we flew in. They played 'Waltzing Matilda' again and did a much better job this time. So there we are with all these kids who might want to do science some day, and this Petco geologist starts yelling and Stephanie Kirsten starts asking me all these embarrassing questions. Of course, the kids all gathered around to hear what I had to say and all I had to say was that we screwed up pretty bad. I wouldn't have minded it so much if it wasn't for the kids. When it gets right down to it, Pres, kids are the only hope we've got, and I just showed a whole bunch of them that science really is for nerds. Aye carumba!"

"Good evening to the Matanuska Valley and all you lonelies in the Bush. This is Prester John Riordan with a special emergency edition of 'Trapline.' This time I've got a message from me to a woman named Rachel. I love you, Rachel, and I love the baby too and I want to come home, wherever that is. You can reach me here if you want by calling the KREL Kountry Radio Trapline. That's 746-TRAP, right here on top of the Bodenburg Butte."

My guest that night was the director of the Alaska Department of Fish and Game. We talked about moose, fish, and the subsistence rights of Native people. One of the callers complained about the Natives, another complained about the whites. Danger Dan complained about the lawyers and my guest complained about all the complaints. The only person who didn't complain was the caller who hung up right away. Just a click and a dial tone. That happens sometimes on the radio. It happened a lot that night.

After the show, I stared at the phone for a while, hoping it would ring and not knowing what I would say if it did. Then the phone did ring. I thought it was Rachel, but I was wrong. It wasn't anybody, just a click and a dial tone. A wrong number or a crank call. A few minutes later, it rang again, just a click and a dial tone. Maybe it was some poor fool who'd lived alone too long and had forgotten how to talk to people. How can you forget what you never knew?

The phone rang a third time. This time it was Rachel. "Hi, Pres," she said, as if we'd last talked yesterday. "I've got a friend who lives in the valley who says you wanted to talk to me. It's about time, sweetie. I almost gave up on you."

Her voice was warm and sleepy. A baby started to cry. I was so nervous I couldn't sit down, so I put our call on the Speakerphone. She was working down in Juneau as some sort of political lobbyist for the Alaska salmon industry. A friend of a friend of a friend had told her about my "Trapline" message. She refused to tell me her friend's name, but I'll always suspect that it was the Speaker's wife. I walked in a circle and talked in a square while the KREL Kountry Komputer played all the latest hits from San Antonio.

"I'm sorry."

"I love you."

"Please forgive me."

"Let's try it again, okay, and we'll get it right this time."

Her voice filled the studio, and her face filled my mind as she told me all about it. It was a baby girl—seven pounds, eleven ounces with gray eyes, rosebud lips, and no hair to speak of. "The doctor says she's a hurtler. She's always crashing into things, like a stunt-girl in a baby movie."

She told me to say something, then put the phone to my daughter's ear. For some reason I don't understand, my voice went up an octave and I babbled like a fool. "I love you, you big baby. That's right, you're a wonderful girl. *Ooobee goobee doobee yabadoo.*"

I'd intended to say something more profound, but never had the chance. Someone was knocking on my door.

"Hang on, okay?" I said. "There's somebody at the door."

It was Dr. Godwin. She said, "I heard your message, Mr. Riordan. It was very touching, I'm sure. Most women would fall for it, but not me. Have you seen my brother Frankie around?"

I took Rachel off the Speakerphone and picked up the receiver. "Who's that?" she said. "It's awfully late to be gathering news."

"This isn't news. This is something else. I'll tell you about it later. Can I call you back in a little while? Ten minutes at the most."

Dr. Godwin was dressed in tailored combat fatigues

—*Cosmo* goes hunting. She adjusted her hips in a threatening manner. "So where is that little twit Frankie? I want those sun pictures back."

I told her I didn't know, and she told me a sad story about growing up in a family of small-time criminals. I think the "small-time" is the part she didn't like. "Frankie really believes that Irish rebel twaddle, that stealing is a political act as long as you steal from an Englishman. The poor boy's daft, I'm afraid. It's all that surfing he did. Too much saltwater and sun on the brain. He wears the Stain as if it were a bleeding badge of honor."

"The Stain? What's that?"

She started to walk around the studio. The clacking of her hunting boots played backbeat to a song of country love by a band called the Cowboy Junkies. "The Stain is what respectable people call Australia's past—the fact that Oz used to be a penal colony. Frankie's proud of the Stain. So tell me, Mr. Riordan, where did Frankie go?"

"I don't know, like I said before. Now I'm afraid you'll have to excuse me. I need to make a telephone call."

"Yes, of course. Ten minutes at the most. Isn't that what you said?"

Dr. Godwin left and I put Rachel back on the Speakerphone, so her voice could fill my life. She gave me the third degree and made me describe my emotions. The trouble with women is, they have all these interesting feelings about almost everything. They expect men to have interesting emotions too, and are always disappointed when we don't. She was fascinated by the Gripper, and his unnatural appetites. Dr. Godwin excited her animosity, and Frankie's quest for his heroic ancestor nearly moved her to tears. She was worried about Dr. Bud and angry at the way he'd been treated on the front page of the *Matanuska News-Nugget*. She admired the Speaker's courage and said a prayer for Sir John Franklin.

"He must have been a very brave man to have listened to his wife like that. Only the strong can be tender, even if he was a bit of a fool. How did you feel when you saw his body floating into the sea?"

I thought about it for a moment, in the hope that some sort of interesting emotion would present itself to me. "Well, I guess I—"

That's when the door crashed open, and Donald Montague's wide shoulders filled up the empty frame. He still had the practical revolver that came with his Survive Pak. He pointed it at me. "Hello, sport," he said. "Who you talking to?"

I told him I was talking to myself. Rachel held her breath on the Speakerphone while Emilou Harris sang a song about some good-looking cowboy who drank too much and loved too little. Dr. Godwin followed Donald through the door.

She said, "Cut the horseshit, Mr. Riordan. I need to know where my brother's hiding out. Donnie says that you're his chum, so you must know where he is."

Donald cracked his knuckles, as if preparing them for action.

"How long have you two been partners?" I said.

Dr. Godwin said "Hush!" but Donald didn't hear her. "We been partners ever since the penny when I was Frankie's cellmate. I tried to find out where Maggie's letter was, but Frankie'd never tell me. He should have told me way back then. It would have saved us all a lot of trouble."

I said, "You're making a big mistake, Donnie. She'll take all the goods and you'll get all the trouble. She sent her own brother to the penny, and she'll do the same to you."

He tried to think about this, but Dr. Godwin wouldn't let him. "Step on his face," she said. "That'll get him started."

Rachel hung up her telephone. The dial tone sounded like an air raid siren when amplified over the Speakerphone. Donald twirled around on his heels, looking for something to shoot. "What's that?" he said.

I gave them some technical gobbledygook. "Audio feedback reverberation." I flipped a switch and the siren stopped. Emilou Harris had finished her song and Karen Wilson, the overnight heartthrob of Kountry Klassics, Inc., was talking about the benefits of a revolutionary new product that did amazing things for wrinkled jowls.

"I really don't know where Frankie is."

Donald said, "Well, the plane we were in is over at the airport, so he must be around here someplace."

I put on my thoughtful face, playing for time as long as I could. When they were all out of patience I said, "Well, if the plane really is at the airport, then maybe I do know where Frankie is."

CHAPTER 26

Donald took the wheel of a rented Bronco and I sat in the passenger's seat. Dr. Godwin sat in back and curled into a shadow so that all that I could see were the flickering whites of her eyes. Trooper Kornvalt was waiting for us at the bottom of the Bodenburg Butte. Donald became quite nervous. Dr. Godwin told him not to be.

"Everything okay, Riordan?" Trooper Kornvalt said. "Dispatch got a call about you all the way from Juneau. A woman name of Rachel says you're in a jam."

"No problem here," I said. "We're headed over to the gravel pit. I've got some new recruits for Danger Dan."

The white snow and the blue moon gave Danger Dan's gravel pit a soft, hazy glow that was totally at odds with the character of the place, which was well armed and fortified. A sign at the end of his driveway proclaimed it to be:

FORT ALASKA

LAST REDOUBT OF THE FREEHOLDERS OF AMERICA

LAWYERS WILL BE SHOT ON SIGHT

The driveway was blocked with a heavy chain of the sort a battleship might use to lower its anchor. "We'll have to walk from here," I said.

Donald asked, "What do you mean walk?"

"Let's get to it, then," Dr. Godwin added.

We stepped around the chain and took three steps before a big voice said, "Halt! Who goes there?"

Dr. Godwin straightened her shoulders and tilted her head at an especially arrogant angle. "Dr. Beverly Godwin, Ph.D. I'm looking for Frankie Stubbs."

The voice took shape. It was Hans Kugler, the assistant fire chief. He said, "Freeholder Stubbs is one among the chosen. Did you know that he's been screwed by lawyers on two continents?"

"No, I didn't know that," Dr. Godwin said. "Tell him his sister wants to have a chat."

Frankie and the Canadian pilot were both wearing the uniform of the Alaska Free Party: heavy work-boots, a lumberjack shirt, and blue jeans rolled up at the cuffs. Frankie also wore a Peterbilt baseball cap. His lumberjack shirt was unbuttoned so that I could read the words inscribed on his T-shirt: COURT OF LAST RESORT. He and the pilot sat at a card table in a smoke-filled room. Danger Dan and a group of his followers were standing around the room. Their hands were all smeared with printer's ink.

The young thief greeted us all in turn, "Donald.

Pres. Hello, sis. I see everybody's working late to-night. I guess there's lots of work to do. Our dear host Dan here is printing another one of his newspapers. It's a funny little sheet he's got. *Kill All the Lawyers,* it's called. I wonder if anybody reads it."

"I'm sure not," Dr. Godwin said. "Now, Franklin, I want you to listen to me. I think we should set things square. It could get very sticky if we don't. Donald here will tell the blues that you forged these so-called letters from Sir John to Maggie Stubbs. Without the letters you're nothing but a thief who's put himself in a serious pickle."

Donald said, "I'll say we cooked it up together when we was in the penny."

"But the letter's genuine."

Donald handled this one: "And sooner or later the blues'll figure that out. But you'll be an old fart by then, and that's no good to anybody. I say it's better to live rich than die rich. You don't want to waste your life with courts and barristers."

Danger Dan said, "He's got a point there, Frankie. Once they get those pictures in court the lawyers'll get all the money."

Frankie got up and walked around the room. Danger Dan gave Donald a manly hug and said, "I like the way you think, son. Have you ever been in jail?"

Frankie said, "All right, sis. Let's talk a deal. I'll share my goods if you share yours, starting with that book you said you wanted to write. How much money will a book fetch if my name's on it too?"

CHAPTER 27

The winters aren't so bad in Juneau. It rains a lot, but the warm currents of the Pacific Ocean keep things from getting too cold. It's a lot like Seattle would be if Seattle had very few people, no highways, and six-hundred-pound rats. Juneau's rats aren't rats, but brown bears that have become addicted to human garbage. The bears are destroyed if they become too bold in their search for leftover bean sprouts and cocktail cheese. Juneau is a very upscale place, at least by Alaskan standards.

We have a lemon yellow house on Star Hill which overlooks a downtown that was built on tailings from an old gold mine that were dumped into Gastineau Channel. The old gold mine haunts the city like an unsolved murder, but that's another story which I cannot tell right now.

The sun pictures surfaced on two occasions. The second was during pledge week for APB, Alaska Public Broadcasting. After thinking about it some more and letting the dust settle a bit, "Science Today" decided to do their documentary after all. A panel of local experts was gathered to talk about the exciting discoveries the Australian group had made. Dr. Bud was invited to be on the panel. He seemed very pleased with himself and talked about Dr. Godwin and her sun pictures for a very long time.

They had a prominent place in the "Science Today" special, as did the lovely Dr. Godwin. The camera lingered on her every curse at every opportunity. The narrator seemed to think that she'd recovered the Holy Grail and chanted her praises in a deep but unhurried radio voice:

> Her quest was like his quest . . . the search for a North-west Passage of the mind . . . where ideas are brought to life by the courage of the people who think them.

That's when they rolled the closing credits, and a fat guy with a bald head and a big gray beard asked us to send some money. Rachel sent them fifteen dollars over my objection. Three weeks later they sent us a public-TV coffee mug on which was emblazoned a subtle appeal for additional funds.

That was the second time I saw the sun pictures. The first time was on a Sunday afternoon, in our lemon yellow house on Star Hill.

The Speaker and Emily were in the habit of visiting us on Sunday afternoons so they could play with our daughter. The Speaker said that she made him feel young, but I suspect she made him feel that old was worth all the trouble. I would sit around in sweatpants and a T-shirt and not even bother to shave. Rachel would sit at the kitchen table and write diatribes against the oil industry while leading a discussion of the usual Sunday topics: politics, religion, and who was sleeping with whom in the Alaska Legislature. The Speaker and I disagreed on almost everything.

But one Sunday we didn't talk about sex, religion, or politics because the Speaker had brought along faxed copies of two pages of an Australian tabloid newspaper that no one dared to believe. This was courtesy of a computerized news service which the

Speaker used to keep an eye on every English-language paper in the world with more than five thousand subscribers. "It's a snap," he said, "All you have to do is go over to the House computer and punch in a few key words. Every Friday, just on a whim, I do data search on Sir John Franklin. This week I found something."

The first page was fast food for thought—big black headlines wrapped around a picture of a size-10 girl in a size-8 bathing suit: DIETARY ADVICE FROM THE *SPORTS ILLUSTRATED* GIRLS . . . 100-YEAR-OLD MAN EATS RATS FOR BREAKFAST . . . MEL GIBSON POINTS PERCY AT ITALIAN STARLET . . . LADY DI'S HAIRDRESSER KNOWS FOR SURE . . . TWO OZZIES TURN FROZEN FRANKLIN INTO COLD, HARD CASH —Illustrated with authentic photographs on page 12!

The sun pictures had been enlarged and enhanced so that faces could be seen on the three men who had planted the Union Jack on King William Island. The man in the middle had fat cheeks and a pear-shaped body, just like the corpse we'd exhumed from the permafrost. He was identified in the caption as Sir John Franklin. The story read as follows:

London's Fleet Street is all in a tizzy about the crash hot deal that's just been made by the brother-sister team of Franklin and Beverly Stubbs. A major British publishing house will shell out some heavy poundage for the rights to their fascinating story.

Mr. Stubbs describes himself as "a man of opportunity" while his sister, the former Mrs. Godwin, has credentials as a scientist. Last year they cooperated in a venture that led to the recovery of valuable artifacts from Sir John Franklin's fatal 1847 voyage in the Polar Sea up north of Canada. The two claim to be the illegitimate progeny of Sir John Franklin, the famous explorer and one-time naval governor of the penal colony of Tasmania.

There are some who would dispute their claim, but there's no quibbling about the remarkable artifacts they recovered from the frozen ground of King William Island.

"These 'sun pictures' are invaluable," said Kinsley Crawford, an expert in such things. "I understand that the Stubbses have already received certain proposals for the purchase of these artifacts."

These "sun pictures," which are reprinted elsewhere on this page, are being held as evidence in criminal proceedings against Donald Montague, a convicted felon from Sydney. He is charged with kidnapping, theft, extortion, assault, and criminal mischief involving a corpse. The Stubbses claim he stole Sir John's body and attempted to steal their valuable "sun pictures." His trial will begin Monday in Vancouver.

"I feel sorry for old Donnie," Mr. Stubbs said in an exclusive interview. "Perhaps this will be a lesson to him that crime does not pay—not in Canada, anyway."

The lovely Miss Stubbs has become the darling of high society, or of what passes for such in Oz. She has recently been seen in the company of a certain prosperous bachelor, and is in great demand as a speaker before female organizations.

"I'll do anything I can to make science of interest to the public," Miss Stubbs said in an exclusive interview. "If I have to write a book to do it, then that's what I will do."

The book deal is reportedly worth 4.6 million quid to Franklin and Beverly Stubbs. Negotiations are now in progress for the dramatic movie rights.

I wrote my own version of the same story for the *New York Times,* but some secretary sent it back with a polite but negative reply. I stopped writing news after that. News is written by people who are underpaid and overexcited. I don't want to be that way anymore. I'd rather be overpaid and underworked, so I got a job with the government, as a staff assistant to the Speaker's Special House Committee on Subsistence Fishing Rights. The Speaker leaves me in charge of his mission whenever he goes back home to meet with the voters who congregate at the foot of the Bodenburg Butte.